# HALF FACE

Mara Li

Lands Atlantic PUBLISHING

Half Face
Published through Lands Atlantic Publishing
www.landsatlantic.com

# HALF FACE

# Chapter 1

## The Wait

He has dark tattoos covering almost every inch of his visible body, including his face, where the ink forms a terrifying mask: one half black as tar, the other half white like a crescent moon, broken only by thick black lines that run from the bridge of his nose to his temple. The darkness makes his eyes stand out shockingly bright blue.

I turn my eyes away from the photograph, not wanting to catch that gaze. The thought that I will have to see him for real in just a few minutes makes my hands clammy. Right now, Harry Dartes is still in the courtroom, giving his testimony. But he'll be alright; Harry is a big, strong man. I saw a lot of anger in his eyes this morning, when we were welcomed by three court attendants of the Justice House. A lot of anger, but no fear.

I don't know whether *I* will be alright. The nightmares became a recurring dread each night, with the date of the hearing creeping closer. And now I'm finally here, and I wish I had never agreed to this.

The room that I'm waiting in is small, and barely comfortable. I'm sitting in one of the two chairs, braiding my fingers together on the tabletop in front of me. There's a cup of cold tea next to me; I have barely sipped from it. The other chair is occupied by a currently silent court attendant.

I don't like the room. I hate the silence.

Somewhere down the hall, I hear the faint noise of a door opening and closing. I look up expectantly, but the court attendant shakes her head.

'You're due 3 at o'clock; don't count on anything earlier. Do you want more tea?' she adds, dropping that brisk tone, as if she suddenly remembers that I am not the one on trial today. I'm just one of the few lucky ones to survive the robbery of Fallhallow National Bank, on the day that the criminal ring, led by their leader known as the Half Face, decided to try their  luck there. The silence, the empty room, they're all just to guarantee a fair trial – or so they've told me. They wouldn't want any of the witnesses to be influenced before giving their testimony in court. Personally, I can't imagine why it would matter. The Half Face was caught with the  blood of his victims still on his hands. I'd seen it myself, just as I had seen the woman whose blood it was tumble to the ground.

'No, thank you,' I mutter, shifting in my chair, uncomfortably aware that my clothes are clinging to my back. I'm wearing a knee-length skirt and a long-sleeved blouse, the most formal look I could muster with the temperature outside the building rising to tropical standards. Even here in this room, hidden away between cold stone hallways and marble pillars, the heat seems to make gravity feel thicker.

I glance at my watch. Fifteen minutes to go. It seems both too fast and too slow.

I go over the rehearsed words in my head. What if I forget everything I need to say? What if I black out, or cry? I don't want to cry where he can see me. No, that cannot happen.

In an attempt to distract myself, I slide my phone out

of my pocket and mindlessly scroll through the menu. I freeze when I come across the news feed.

*Liveblog: trial of top-criminal known as "the Half Face" continuing today.*

Someone in that courtroom is twittering the events, and I'm locked up in this miserable room until they can bring me out like the next circus act.

'I must ask you to put your phone away for now,' the woman says. When I look up, I find her looking at me with a pitying gaze. 'We don't want you to read anything that can influence your statement.'

Of course. 'I'm just nervous,' I say, and put my phone back in my pocket.

'You will be absolutely fine. If you find you don't want to look at him, you don't have to. Remember that you're doing this to help us put him away for good. That is why you chose to testify, isn't it?'

'Right.'

She nods, and we fall into silence again, until there's a brief knock on our door. The woman smiles, rises from her chair and beckons me.

Suddenly, my heart is racing even harder than before. 'Can...can I go to the bathroom real quick?'

'Sure. Just this way.' She leads me over to another

door and remains outside as I enter.

The tiles are shiny and clean. I hear the buzzing of air conditioning.

After I flush, I take a quick moment to splash a handful of cold water in my face. It helps a little. I lean my hands on the sink and stare at my reflection in the round mirror. I'm very pale. My eyes are wide open, like a frightened animal. Strands of dark brown hair are falling from the bun that had been so tightly secured this morning. They cling to my sweaty face. I brush them away.

The woman knocks on the door. 'Juliet? It's time.'

I'm on the verge of calling out: *No! Leave me alone, I'm not going!* There's a thick feeling in my throat that I try to get rid of by swallowing. When it doesn't work, I settle for a deep breath before wiping my palms on my skirt and exiting the bathroom.

'There's no need to be nervous,' the woman says again. But what does she know? She didn't have to drop to the ground, pretending to be a dead body, while a monster was standing mere feet away from her barking orders.

We make our way across the building, all the way to the end of the long corridor, and make a right turn. The entire building is so *clean*. We pass a large, square painting on the wall; we pass a mirror where I briefly catch my pale reflection, we pass a man with a cell phone pressed to his ear, giving us a curious glance.

Then the woman stops in front of a dark, polished door. The small plate next to the door reads *Courtroom 14.*

We're here.

The woman gives me an encouraging smile. I pull up the corners of my mouth, just enough to make it look like I'm smiling back.

'Remember, you just have to answer a few questions. I'll be here to escort you back.'

'I know.'

She looks like she wants to say something else, but before she does, the door opens. I automatically step back, creating some space for Harry Dartes. He sees me, undoubtedly registers the worry in my eyes, and gives my shoulder a brief squeeze. 'It's worse just before you go in, girl.'

I nod. He smiles one last time before another court attendant urges him on, and mine gestures to me, indicating that I will have to enter Courtroom 14 at last.

I check my posture, make sure my shoulders are straight and my jaw is set. Then I relax my fists, which I'm clenching without really noticing it.

'Good luck,' the woman says.

And then I take a step inside. The door closes behind me.

# Chapter 2

## Testimony

I have only a few short seconds to take in my new surroundings.

The room is much smaller than I had imagined. A man in a black robe is sitting behind a bench on a dais. That's the judge, of course, and the woman in the middle of the room must be the prosecutor. The jury is on my far left side and then there are a couple of people in the gallery at the other side of the room. Journalists, I am guessing. One of them is tweeting the live blog. I can already imagine what he is writing: *Witness number 3 has just entered the hearing. She looks like she is about to puke.*

'Right this way, Miss Cunningham,' says another woman, taking over the job of my previous attendant and leading me to a place between the judge and the jury. I mutter a thank-you and sit down, uneasily aware that all eyes are turned to me. I swallow, and slowly turn my own eyes to where I irrevocably will have to look.

He is sitting far away from me, almost at the other side of the courtroom. The only person next to him is a pretty woman in her mid-thirties. His attorney, I realize. I'm confused to see a flushed look on her face when she leans close to him as he mutters something in her ear. She nods, then leaves him sitting there, all on his own, while she takes her own place close to the prosecutor.

Suddenly, his eyes flash away from her and lock with mine. I'm caught off-guard, not quick enough to look away. He is closer to me now than he was in Fallhallow National Bank and I can see him very well. His tattooed face is a perfect yin and yang. My mouth dries up.

'Our third witness today is Miss Juliet Eva Cunningham. Born on the third of October, 1994. Miss Cunningham, are these facts correct?'

I need a moment to realize that the person speaking is waiting for my answer. The mouth of the Half Face lifts up in a lazy smile as I tear my gaze away, feeling the heat rise to my cheeks. He can't move, I remind myself, steadying my breath. Even if he fights, he can't break free of those handcuffs. 'Yes. Ma'am.'

'Alright then, Miss Cunningham,' says the prosecutor. 'I will be asking you a few questions during this hearing. Please listen well, and answer with as much detail as you can remember. It is important that you state only what you can remember. If you feel that you cannot clearly recall something, you should tell us so rather than express your best guess. Is anything unclear at this point?'

I shake my head.

She gives me the tiniest of smiles. 'Then we'll proceed.' She pauses to straighten her microphone. 'Miss Cunningham, you were present during the entire robbery of Fallhallow National Bank.'

This is a fact that hardly needs acknowledgment, but I still nod and squeak out a weak, 'yes.'

'Can you tell me what you were doing at said place at that time of day?'

I lick my dry lips. I will have to speak now, and it feels like there is a whole bucket of sand in my throat. 'I needed stamps,' I croak, realizing that I'm barely audible at all. I clear my throat and try again. 'The bank has a post office. I'd been sent to buy thirty sheets of stamps, for letters to the parents. The…the kids have head lice.'

'You mean the children of the Expedition Fallhallow Elementary School, where you are currently doing an internship.'

'Yes, ma'am.'

'And how long had you been inside when you noticed the first signs of an attack?'

'I…I think it must have been five minutes.'

'Now, Miss Cunningham, can you give me an account of what transpired from the moment that the attackers entered the building?'

'I don't know when they entered,' I say truthfully. 'I think…maybe they were inside before I got there. But I heard screaming, and people suddenly panicked, so I looked around and heard the gunshots.' My voice falters.

'What did you see at that point?' the prosecutor urges me on. 'Take your time to think.'

I brave another look at the Half Face. I can't tell if he is listening to my words or not. He doesn't look so worried. He looks quite relaxed actually, stretching his legs in front of him as if this courtroom is his home; as if he's simply watching something mildly interesting.

It's not just his face that is tattooed. He has the same black ink on his broad arms. It reaches down to his wrists, like tattooed sleeves without warmth. The war paint doesn't end there: ornate symbols adorn the knuckles of his  hands, which he now puts in front of him awkwardly, the handcuff giving him little room to move.

I stare at those hands.  The hands that  choked  the woman with the blond braid and pulled the trigger of that jet black gun.

*No, you can't let him distract you. Focus on the question, Juliet,* I tell myself sternly.

I had only dropped by the stately bank in the middle of town because it has a post office, and it was closest to the elementary school where I had just started my internship. My first day, a scorching 29 degrees Celsius, and me a bundle of nerves. Before I'd had the chance to come face to face with the group I would be teaching, before I could even be introduced to all of the staff in the teachers' room, someone had stuffed a few coins into my sweaty palm. *Go buy stamps,* they'd told me. *Make sure you get, like, thirty sheets; we need to send out letters. The kids have head lice.*

I'd been scratching my own head during my entire walk down to the bank.

And then, the world had just shattered. The humid air pierced by the high-pitched screaming of a woman, followed  by a pandemonium of voices, and a rush of people trying to get to the exit. Their feet had made the floor of Fallhollow National Bank vibrate, like an earthquake. For a moment, I had really believed it *was* an earthquake.

Then something had exploded close to my ear, and the high-pitched screaming had stopped so abruptly that I'd automatically turned my head to see where the woman had gone.

On her belly, as it had turned out, with her arms spread out. The floor around her had been weirdly red, and wet, and she had been very still.

As I recount all of these things aloud in the courtroom, my voice seems strangely distant. I can hear myself as though I'm an outsider.

'Did he shoot this woman directly, Miss Cunningham?' asks the prosecutor, interrupting the images that flash before my eyes.

Recalling the look on her face as the woman crumpled to the ground ignites a spark of angry courage in me. I turn my head to glare at the Half Face, who is still looking at me with that lazy smile. 'You would have to ask *him* that,' I say venomously.

'But what was your perception?'

'He shot her and she fell down at once.'

The woman nods. 'What did you do then?'

'I was scared.' Slowly, I had started to comprehend what was going on. What the loud banging noises all around me had meant. What was being shouted at us in a rain of commands: *get down on the floor now!*

I'd dropped down next to the dead woman, just in time to avoid two men brushing past me, both with loaded guns pointing at something – some*one* – that I hadn't seen.

I had covered my head with my arms and had tried not to breathe at all, while the blood was rushing in my ears just like the questions that were tumbling through my mind like a storm. Was this a robbery? An attack – Jihad? I had not even been sure what the attackers looked like, how many of them had been there, or if someone had been pointing a gun at me. I'd have had to look up in order to figure all of that out, which meant having to move, and I couldn't have thought of anything that I'd desired less. My whole body had been weak from fear.

But then, I'd heard *his* voice. It was a raspy, unpolished sound, which carried through the entire building. The sound had seemed to originate from somewhere left of the dead woman, eerily close to where I had been pretending to be shot.

"I'm here to make a la-a-a-arge withdrawal," the voice

had said. "No? Aw, come now, Fallhollow bankers! One of you will have to do it. You see, this is a game-*ah*!" The way he said it made the last consonant bounce. When nothing had happened, I'd heard a chuckle. "You mean I get to choose? Why, thank you, gen-tle-*men*. Okay, alright, I'm gonna pick – *you* live, *you* die."

Immediately after: the sound of a gun being fired; close, too close to me. It left a beeping sound in my left ear. When that beeping sound had faded, I had registered heavy footsteps circling me and the nameless woman beside me, pausing just once.

I had been breathing shallowly for long minutes, dying to take a full breath of air. The footsteps continued. I had opened my mouth, inhaling the air as quietly as possible.

With the new breath had come a little bit of new courage, and I had gingerly lifted my head just high enough that I could see over my own arms. The floor had been scattered with people. Some were still sitting. Others didn't move at all.

I had watched a handful of masked men run around with large bags, but my attention had been drawn to the silent figure standing in the middle of the hall.

I had known, without doubt, that it had been *his* footsteps that I had heard. That the raspy voice belonged to him.

The man had glanced sideways, and I thought that he had been wearing a mask like the others, covering up all the features of his face. Even when he moved, I'd thought that his mask had been somehow torn, because the other half of his face had been clearly visible, even if it was ghostly white.

It felt like hours that I had stared at that face, too transfixed and too horrified to remember to lower my head again. Finally, I had realized that I was not staring at a tattered mask, but that the face of the man before me was all solid ink.

That face set him apart from the common species of man. It had made him a monster.

The smile on that same face dies away when I finish that last thought aloud, and my voice trails off. Even though the Half Face is cuffed and guarded, I feel exposed to danger.

*Don't be a coward now, Juliet. You chose to see him today. Besides, this isn't Fallhallow Bank. We're safe in here – I'm safe in here.*

Still, my heart is hammering away in my chest. I want to rush out of the courtroom now that I've told my story, run down the stairs and make my way home. Why should I testify that this man, this monster, shot a dozen people with a smile on his face? He doesn't even want to deny it.

The Half Face moves in his chair, whispering something to his attorney. Before she can give a reply, I'm startled to hear his voice, well audible in the silent courtroom. It's as raspy and low as I remember. 'I would just like to say, *Juliet*, that I'm not a monster. I'm not-*ah*.'

I stare at him, my mouth hanging slightly open. Is he allowed to talk to me?

'I would ask you to refrain from speaking at this time, sir,' the judge says at once, answering my question.

'I think *Juliet* should understand –'

'Sir, you will have a chance to speak later.'

The Half Face leans back in his chair, his eyes steadily on me. He doesn't speak anymore, but his smile doesn't return either.

'Please, tell us what happened after the masked men had obtained the money from the bank,' asks the prosecutor. She sounds unperturbed, as if the Half Face has not interrupted us and turned my cheeks scarlet.

I collect my thoughts. 'He...The Half Face, he told the others to go. Then he – he bowed.'

'Did he or his men shoot any more people on their way out?'

'Not that I could tell with my head down.'

The prosecutor nods. 'What did you do after they had left?'

'I waited until the other survivors started talking,' I admit, remembering how I had remained quietly on the floor, my limbs too weak to move properly. I had tasted vomit in my mouth. 'By the time I stood up, Harry – Mister Dartes – had called 911.'

'Were you familiar with Mister Dartes at that time?'

'No, he just took care of me. He is the strongest one.'

'Miss Cunningham, thank you.' The prosecutor smiles at me. 'I have no more questions.'

Relief washes over me, and for the first time I find that I'm able to relax my muscles. 'Can I leave now?'

'You may.'

My attendant on this side of the door crosses over to where I'm sitting. I stand up, following him to the polished door. My heart settles into its usual steady rhythm. I've done it – I got through the hearing without crying, and I will never have to see that black-and-white mask again. Maybe the nightmares won't visit me tonight.

Before I can step out, I hear his voice trailing after me: '*Ju*-lie, where're you going?'

A shiver runs down my spine, but I don't stop. Two seconds later, my attendant closes the door and I am out in the hallway, where the air conditioner blows cold air in my face.

# Chapter 3

## Taken

I'm taken back to that same glum waiting room where I began. While I was in the courtroom, someone must have come and removed the untouched cup of tea, because it is no longer there. Without sitting down, I turn to my attendant. 'Am I allowed to go home?'

'Not yet,' he says. 'There's some information we need you to fill in. If you could wait here, I will get you the forms. It will take only a minute or two,' he adds, seeing my face fall into an exhausted expression. 'You have been brave, Juliet. Facing him today is what will help us remove him from society for a long time.'

I nod and lower myself onto the chair. The attendant walks out, leaving the door open a crack. I wonder what is going to happen to the Half Face now. I'm not a doctor, but this guy seems to have a few bolts and screws loose. Maybe I should stick around and hear the conviction. But no. I'm too tired, and the hearing might go on for hours. It doesn't matter anyway; it will be all over the news eventually.

I remember my phone, stuffed away in the pocket of my skirt, and pull it out.

For the first time this day, I manage a real smile. The liveblog is describing most of my testimony, including me leaving the room and the judge's decision to take a ten minute recess.

I decide to send a text message to my mom. She'd wanted to come with me today, but I had told her no. I couldn't really explain it then, and I can't quite explain it now. Maybe I just needed to look the Half Face in the eyes on my own, just like I had been alone in the hall of Fallhallow National Bank.

*I'll be coming home soon,* I type out on my phone and press send.

It only takes a few seconds for a reply to show up on the screen: *Did it go well? Are you alright, sweetheart?*

*Yes, things are good. See you soon. X*

I put my phone back in my pocket and drum on the tabletop with my fingers. What's taking the attendant so long retrieving a couple of forms? I get up and cross the entire room, which only takes four steps. The hallway outside is deserted.

A shrill noise pierces the solemn quiet of the Justice Hall. It's a high-pitched and penetrating sound, like a fire alarm. I jump. My nerves – still not completely calm anyway – are immediately back on edge. I step out of the room and scan the corridor left and right. Is there a fire somewhere? I can't see anything out of the ordinary, but what else could have caused the alarm to go off so suddenly?

The noise just keeps screeching, coming towards me from all directions. I cast another nervous look around, but there's still no sight of my attendant. Should I stay and wait for him to give me instructions? But what if there really is a fire somewhere close? I could get trapped. There's only a little window in the waiting room, and it's far too small for me to climb through in case of an emergency.

I will just go down to the lobby, where security searched me before I was allowed to enter the main building. Surely, someone there will be able to tell me what's going on. I think I remember the way.

I start to make my way down the corridor, when the alarm bells stop as abruptly as they had started. Automatically, I slow down, listening to the dead silence. My ears stop ringing and I hear two female voices calling something to each other somewhere up ahead. I can't understand what they're saying, but they sound rather shrill. Another voice joins them, booming a command. The two women don't reply and the alarm doesn't go off again.

There's a few seconds in which I think that everything is back to normal. Then, the lights in the corridor go out without a warning. I am left in complete darkness, with only a faint glow ahead of me. Now I really stop walking, trying to take in the shadows. What the hell is going on? A power outage? My heart starts thumping in my throat.

A door opens and closes softly, only a little way ahead of me. There's just enough light for me to see a silhouette of a person emerging from the doorway, pausing.

'I'm sorry...I think there's something wrong with the power,' I say hesitantly.

'Yeah, something's up,' the person replies.

Relief washes over me. For some reason I was afraid, but now it dawns on me how ridiculous that was. If this isn't the safest building in Fallhallow, then what is? I smile and approach the other person, a lawyer or another court attendant, coming out of his office to see what the fuss and the noise is all about. 'Can you help me? I was supposed to wait, but my attendant never returned. I'm not sure where I'm supposed to go, but I would like to go home as soon as...'

Something about his stance sets off a warning bell in my head. He is still hard to make out in the shadows, but I can see that he has very broad shoulders, now slightly hunched, like he is trying to make himself smaller than he actually is, and that he is cocking his head slightly to the left, as if he's trying to hear if something is happening in the corridors ahead of us, while also keeping his attention fixed on me.

I feel coldness spread from my abdomen to every part of my body. *But it can't be, it's impossible –*

He breaks away from the doorway and makes a few relaxed, almost casual steps in my direction. I can hear that he drags his left foot over the floor; slowly, then his right, then his left again.

'I can help you, Julie.'

That low rasp in his voice punches me in the face like a fist. For a few seconds I am too shocked to move, or even to wonder how it is possible that a man who was handcuffed in the courtroom just minutes ago is now standing in front of me. He takes those few seconds to eliminate the distance between us, until his face becomes visible, and I can distinguish those sharp eyes staring down at me.

'You...you...you're not supposed to be here,' I stammer.

'Who told you that?' he asks, a certain relish still clear in his voice, even though he tones down the volume to match my own breathy, faltering sound. 'Because you see, Jools, according to *my* plan, I'm definitely supposed to be here.'

*Scream, Juliet!*

'SOMEONE HELP M –' My cry is cut off by his hand clamping down on my mouth, his fingertips sinking into my cheek.

'Somebody help her, help her!' he mimics a panicky voice, not loud enough for anyone but me to hear. The next moment, I feel myself being whipped around by my shoulders, so he is standing behind me and he can wrap his free arm around my waist. I'm shocked when my body slams directly into his. 'Please, don't scream, Juliet. The good folks of the Justice House might think you're in *trouble*.'

While he talks, I feel his warm breath tickling my neck. His tight grip, and the sheer dread that spins my head, make me freeze on the spot. He shifts behind me, slipping his hand to my lower arm and wrenching it behind my back painfully. I let out a gasp.

'Hush,' he mutters. I hear a metallic click. Something cold presses against the sensitive skin of my throat; the blade of a knife that is so sharp that I'm scared it will cut me open if I only breathe too hard.

'You can scream now,' he says, and his hand disappears from my mouth. When I don't respond at once, he presses the knife closer to my throat. 'C'mon, *really* let it out. SCREAM!' he yells in my ear.

I open my mouth and shriek. 'HELP ME! PLEASE!'

The Half Face's rough laugh mixes with my cries. 'That's a good girl.'

# Chapter 4

## For money or a principle

I don't have to scream for long. Before I can count to ten, the corridor is invaded by security guards from the Justice House, pulling out their guns. I don't know what frightens me more; the iron grip of the Half Face on my waist, or seeing those weapons being pointed at my heart.

'Stand down!' one of the guards barks.

The Half Face lets out another savage laugh; I feel it vibrating through my own body. 'No no *no*, gentlemen; this is not how it works! You see, *you* have nothing. I have everything. Every-tiny-bit of leverage.' As if to prove it, he weaves one hand through my hair and pulls back hard, forcing my head back with a snap. I let out an unwanted groan of pain.

'Leave the girl,' the security guard says. 'Let her go now, and we can talk this through in a civilized manner.'

'You're not getting THE IDEA!' the Half Face bellows. 'This is *me* calling the shots and *you* stupid oafs standing down, or the girl dies a tragic death. You see, Jools,' he mutters, suddenly quietly, pressing his mouth into my hair, 'Do you see how they're simply risking your life to keep me contained? Is that fair to you, huh? Is it?'

I have to blink hard against the tears if I want to see what is going on around me. 'Please don't shoot,' I whisper at the guards. I don't want to die, one way or another. God, I just want to go home.

'We're not shooting.' Even with the painful angle my head is in, I can make out that the man lowers his gun. My heart lifts, but I'm too quick.

'Hand me the gun,' the Half Face says. 'GIVE IT!'

'I don't think –'

'No, you don't. Because if you *did*, ah, well, you know what would happen to little Julie here.'

I suddenly feel something warm and hot in the nape of my neck, followed by a burning pain. I realize that the Half Face is sliding that knife of his across my throat. I start shaking in silence, too scared to even whimper.

'Tick...tock,' he says slowly.

'Just stop. I'm giving you the gun.'

'Good man. Put it there, on the floor.' The burning sensation immediately stops and my head is released. Everyone watches as the first security guard carefully sinks to a squatting position, laying down his gun. He pulls his hands away at once, moving back up and taking a step backwards. The others have not yet put away their firearms, I notice, but the guns are pointing downward.

'Julie, you think you can get that for me?' the Half Face asks me conversationally. 'Don't worry – I'm gonna be right behind you.'

I have a thick feeling in my throat, making it almost impossible for me to speak. 'You...want me to get that gun?' I whisper, not entirely sure if I have understood him right.

'You can do that, can't you?'

My head spins as I gingerly take one step forward, then sink to my knees to reach for the weapon with my left hand. The Half Face keeps his grip on my right wrist, squeezing so hard that I can feel a bruise forming there.

The gun is much heavier than I had imagined. I turn back to the Half Face, obediently crossing the distance between us, when I'm struck with a desperate kind of courage. There's no time to figure out if I can pull the trigger without first pulling the safety pin, but I lean in and swing the heavy steel weapon at him, putting my full weight into the blow.

The barrel collides with his jaw, and although he staggers back, he doesn't release his grip on my arm. Quicker than I can collect my wits, he yanks the gun from my hand, turns me around so that I smash against his body once again, and delivers a fist-punch to my belly. I double up, coughing. Dozens of black spots explode before my eyes.

'Shouldn't have done that,' I hear him say somewhere above me.

For a while, all I can do is focus on my own breathing, and the searing pain in my stomach. I'm vaguely aware that the Half Face is talking, and that the guards are arguing with him. It doesn't last long; before I know it, I'm yanked up by my arms and shoved into a small chamber; the same room where I sat waiting before I was called out to testify.

I find the chair and sit down on it. I'm not exactly sure to what conclusion the Half Face and the guards have come in the brief moment that I was gasping for air, but I know that it can't be any better than before, seeing as he now has a knife, a hostage and a fully loaded gun.

I look at him as he inspects the weapon, before tucking it into his belt. There's one second in which I wonder if I could be quick enough to reach out and grab it, this time actually pulling the trigger. I imagine how fast it could be over, how happy I'd be... Then I look up to find his gaze fixed on me, his black-and-white face a menacing mask. I don't stand a chance with him looking at me like that, and there's no telling what he'd do to me if I tried.

'Well, you look worried,' he says. 'Is it the ink? You know, there's a story behind that head. You see, my brother and my sister...' His head snaps up, distracted by a new noise out in the hallway. He runs his tongue over his lips. 'Well, you'll hear that some other time.'

'Aren't you going to kill me?' I ask, surprising myself. I feel sick to my stomach, but I just have to ask. If these are going to be my last moments on earth, I might as well know.

'*Kill you*? Why would I do that, Julie? After all the trouble I went through to see you again!'

'What...what do you mean, trouble?'

'I saw you pretending to be dead,' he chuckles softly. 'You were peeping at me from down on the floor.'

He had seen that? I struggle to understand what this means. 'If you knew, why didn't you shoot me?'

He smiles at me as he closes in on my chair. His fingers trail over my cheek. I look away, but am immediately forced to look back at him, those same fingers turning their hold on my face into an iron grip. 'Because you just looked *so* scared. Just like you're doin' now.' He holds my face a little longer before he lets go.

'Is it money?' I ask, clinging to my last strands of hope. 'Are you going to ask for ransom? Because my mother will pay, I promise she will, if you would just tell m –'

'Oh, Juliet; I don't think coins are gonna cut it,' he says, returning to that lopsided smile that he showed me in Courtroom 14. 'Don't look so down. You're gonna see Mommy and Daddy again sometime. Cross my heart.'

*Sometime?* His words should encourage me, but all I feel is a dreadful cold sensation. 'What exactly are you planning?' I ask faintly.

He stares at me with squinting eyes, like he is contemplating his answer. 'I have a...problem-*ah*,' he says, letting the final m bounce on his tattooed lips. 'Now, I know that you *think* you know what it is and that locking me away is going to solve *all the other* troubles, but this is *not* the way. No, it's not-*ah*.'

I shake my head, not even understanding what he is telling me. He either doesn't see my confused look or he chooses to ignore it, because he turns his back on me and walks to the tiny window to peer out. I don't know what's on the other side and his expression doesn't give away anything.

If this is going to take much longer, my heart might just give up from fear. I don't dare to get up from my chair, much less make a run for it with his intimidating presence so close. He could probably tackle me before I even got the chance to reach for the doorknob.

I wrap my arms around my own waist and pull my legs under the chair. The skirt pulls tight against my legs; I feel a hard bump in my pocket. My phone! I'd forgotten that I had it on me.

With another glance at the Half Face, I reach down into my pocket and quickly retrieve the phone, the blood pumping in my ears from excitement. This feels like a small victory.

But now what? Should I call 911? By now, the entire Fallhallow police force must be swarming around the building. With sweaty fingers, I swipe at the menu to get to my text messages. Mom's last message sends a jolt through my heart. Has she already been called by the police? She might be standing just outside the Justice House, sick with worry. All I want now is to hear her voice, telling me that everything is going to be fine...

'You really don't want to do that,' the Half Face's voice says softly. From the warmth of his breath, I can tell that he is standing right behind me. As I automatically whip my head around, he takes the phone from my hand and frowns down on it.

'Give it back. Please.'

'You know how they say that you can tell a lot about a person just by looking at their clothes? That's true for phones as well. I can tell who you are just by looking... at... your...photos.' He flips through the menu as he talks, then holds up the phone to show me that he has indeed found the pictures. I feel strangely violated.

'And who is this *handsome* young chap?'

He's found the picture of me and Christopher. Chris is ruffling my hair and I'm laughing, pretending to push him away. 'No one,' I say stiffly.

His tattooed mouth widens in a grin, and I see a flash of his teeth. 'Now, now, that can't be right. Look at the smoldering look you're giving him! It's alright, Julie, you can tell me if you have a boyfriend.'

'He's not,' I snap, before I can control my tongue. Why

did he have to find *that* picture of all things?

'That is un*for*tunate. Who ended it?'

'He did,' I say angrily.

'Aw, how tragic. I bet that just broke your little heart.'

Yes, it did break my heart. I look away, pressing my lips together. Fortunately, he doesn't get a chance to force the subject, because the little room is filled with the sudden sound of sirens. I jump and automatically stare at the window. The sound seems to be coming from that direction.

'Now, *there's* Fallhallow's Finest,' the Half Face mutters, a grin still on his lips. 'Want to see what's goin' on, Jools? Come take a look.'

I don't want to get closer to him, but he is right: I am desperate to know what is happening outside the Justice House, dying for any sign that rescue is on its way. So I get up and move to the window, pressing my face to the glass. The Half Face is behind me at once, leaning over me.

The window looks out over a square, bordered by trees. I don't recognize the place, but maybe this is the back of the Justice House. A dozen police cars are scattered across the plaza, and I catch glimpses of people in uniform organizing themselves in ways that I can't quite analyze right now. I focus on a man and a woman standing in the middle of the square. They are both wearing military uniforms, and the man is clutching a megaphone.

'Half Face – we know you can hear us. Please come out and talk. I repeat, Half Face…'

'They just don't under*stand* who's giving the orders here,' the Half Face says. He shoves me aside and pushes against the window. It opens to a crack, letting in a waft of moist summer air. 'THE MEGAPHONE CAN SHUT HIS JABBER,' he roars down to the square. It takes a few seconds, then the sirens stop, and the square falls into an eerie silence. 'Good. Now I can talk.'

The man in the middle of the square lowers his megaphone. He looks uncomfortable and a little put-out that he has been interrupted, but the woman's voice is quite steady as she replies: 'Go ahead, Half Face. I hear you.'

'Excellent; now we've all established that we're not *deaf*.' The Half Face raises his hand, holding up one finger in the air. 'I want one man, unarmed, to approach the building, so he can take my...orders-*ah*. One man only, you two understand that, Mister Plod and Mistress Plonk?'

The two turn to each other to argue briefly. Then the woman turns her face to the window again, and nods.

'There's a man coming up.'

The Half Face slips an arm around my shoulders and pulls me to him. 'You see, Julie, asking gets you almost anywhere. Let's go out and meet him, shall we?'

His arm doesn't leave my shoulders as he positions us in the corridor, my side firmly pressed against his. I try to edge away, but his fingers only press harder in the flesh of my upper arm. I wince and hold still.

The silence feels thick; I'm very conscious of my own beating heart, thumping so loudly that I'm pretty sure the Half Face can hear it. Maybe I should say something. Clearly, I don't stand a shred of a chance if it comes to a struggle, but maybe it is possible for me to try and talk my way out...? My mind races for the right thing to say, but before I can come up with something other than a pathetic plea, a different man in military uniform appears at the end of the corridor.

'Time to play,' I hear the Half Face mutter softly before he pulls out his gun and I'm yet again confronted with that horrible feeling of having cold steel being pressed to my neck; only this time my life could be over within less than a heartbeat.

The man spots the gun too. His step falters for a second, then his face sets in an even deeper frown as he slowly comes towards us.

'Ah pa pa, that's far enough, mister,' the Half Face says.

The man immediately stops, raising his empty hands in the air. 'I've come unarmed, as you can see. Can I talk to the girl, please?'

The Half Face makes a non-committal noise. I notice that the man is looking at me as if he's worried that I might shatter any second. I feel oddly better thanks to that – my legs aren't shaking as much as before, though maybe it's just that I am just too numb to feel any more fear.

'Juliet, are you alright? Are you hurt anywhere?'

I shake my head. 'I'm not hurt.'

'Good. You know that everything will be alright, yes? Your mom is waiting for you just outside; we're going to get you back to her safe and sound.'

'You really believe him, Jools?' the Half Face chuckles. 'You think he can make you promises when I AM THE ONE IN CHARGE!' He doesn't wait for an answer, but continues, 'How about some *orders*, hm? How about some negotiations?'

'Alright, Half Face. What about the orders?'

'Okay, here they are. One interpreter. One van – make

it green, I like green, make sure it's green; oh, and throw in a driver. And two plane tickets-*ah.* Don't worry about logistics, you can deliver the van and the interpreter once we get there.'

I feel like I'm falling into a tub of icy-cold water as he rattles off all his demands. Again, I wonder desperately what this man hopes to obtain; he definitely wasn't lying when he told me that he didn't care for ransom. Plane tickets and an interpreter can only mean travel – but... but...*Two* tickets? Surely, he is not going to force me to come with him? That would be absurd! I can't make sense of any of this, and judging by his face, the mediator cannot, either.

'Two plane tickets,' he repeats sharply. 'Where to, exactly?'

'Now, now, don't be like that. Madame Merryman has all the details you'll be needing.'

'Your attorney?'

'My *excellent* attorney. She'll find that a complete list of my needs has just *slipped* into her files.'

'If we can just talk about the position of the girl –'

'Ah, no.'

'We are very worried that Juliet's involvement –'

'Juliet is *my* concern, Mister Plop. You worry your

mustache about getting me everything I just listed, or we might hear some noise today. BANG!' His sudden shout causes me to jerk violently. The Half Face laughs and gives me a squeeze. 'I think we're done-*ah*,' he says.

The man, looking startled, opens his mouth like he wants to object more. I give my head a tiny shake, staring at him. The gun is still pressing against my neck and I don't want to give the Half Face any kind of excuse to pull that trigger.

The man finally seems to give up. He nods, turning around. I have a sinking feeling in my stomach as I realize that he can walk away a free man, while the heavy arms of the Half Face lock me in my place.

'Wait, wait!' The Half Face waves the hand with the gun through the air, stopping the man dead. I grow even more rigid. 'Don't forget the clothes-*ah*,' the Half Face says with a satisfied chuckle. He rests his chin in my hair, bringing his mouth close to my ear. 'It won't be so hot where we're goin'.'

'W...where do you want to go?' I whisper.

'*We* go, snuck-ums. And we're a-goin' to Ulaanbaatar.'

'*What?*' I am so shocked that it drives out the fear.

'Why, has nobody taught you anything about the world?' the Half Face chuckles in my hair. 'And here I thought you were goin' to be a teacher.'

'That's in Mongolia!' I shout at him. 'What the hell is going on? What is *wrong* with you?'

He grabs me, turns me around so that I am facing him, and for a moment I'm confronted with the outrageous anger that disfigures his face. Then my head reels when his hand grabs my neck. Before I can collect myself and raise my arms in defense, I am slammed against the wall, my head hitting the stone hard enough that I black out for a few seconds. In this darkness, I feel his hot breath on my face. His hands close around my windpipe. 'Try a little respect, Juliet,' he growls, somewhere very close.

I gasp, struggling to find a way to resurface, but the darkness only sucks me in more. The last thing I feel is his grip slackening, but then I'm already falling too deep.

# Chapter 5

## What ties us up

There's a throbbing in my head that gets worse with every passing second. It's like someone is hitting me with an enormous hammer, again and again and again. I dimly grow aware of movement around me, slightly shaking me, and I hear the low sound of an engine running.

Something is wrong. I can't quite put my finger on it. Did I have an accident? It would explain the headache. I try to lift my hands, but discover that the movement of my arms is very restricted. I move my legs, but run into the same problem.

'Hey, snoozles,' the Half Face's unpolished voice says.

My eyes snap open at once, and I stare at my surroundings. I'm in the passenger's seat of a spacious car. We're driving fast; where to, I cannot tell. The road ahead is dark, and all I can make out are the headlights casting their yellow beams on the tarmac.

I look at the Half Face, his hands on the wheel, one finger tapping a relaxed rhythm. The white half of his face is turned to me, ghostlike and pale. The other half – the black side – seems to simply melt into the darkness.

'You have been out a lo-o-ong time,' he says. His gaze flashes to meet mine for a moment, then he turns it back to the road.

I say nothing; my mouth is too dry, and anyway, I'm having a hard time coherently stringing together my thoughts. Slowly, I let my eyes wander to my wrists. Now I understand why I can barely move: he has tied my hands together with a thick rope. The same rope is wrapped around my ankles, making it hard for me to even heave myself into a straighter position.

'Say something, Julie. I need to know that you're okay.'

My gaze slowly swerves back from my bound wrists to him. Why is it so hard to think right now? I close my eyes, trying to focus on my breathing. All I can really feel is the pain radiating from my head to the rest of my body. 'I'm not okay,' I finally manage. 'You...you hurt me.'

'I won't have to if you do what I say, Juliet.'

I rest my head against the window. The cold glass eases the pain a little. 'Where are we going?'

'To the airport. In fact, we're almost there. You're not afraid of flying, are you, Julie?'

'Did they just let you drive off?' I had meant to snap at him, but the question sounds more like a pathetic whimper. There are hardly any other cars on the road. Why aren't they chasing us with blaring sirens? Shouldn't they...shouldn't they try to rescue me?

'Oh, they didn't want to. No, no. But then your *mother* stepped up. Said she'd rather see you alive and far away. Said she couldn't bear to have you dead underground.'

'Oh, God.' I let my head slump back against the window again and wish I could go back to being unconscious. The mere thought of my mother, scared and helpless, squeezes my throat and jabs at my heart.

Minutes pass. I watch the lights at the sides of the road as they hit the windows time and again, then quickly trail off behind us. They're like falling stars, and we're a meteorite, racing through a dark universe towards our own destruction.

The Half Face seems comfortable with the silence. He's

humming to himself, his fingers, covered  in ink, still patting that same rhythm on the steering wheel. I take this time to think, trying to reconstruct the last events before I lost consciousness. He must have dragged or carried my limp body downstairs, keeping his gun to my head as he negotiated with the police forces outside on the square. I can just imagine that face, and his grin, baring his teeth, as my mother begged him to let me go. And, when that didn't work and the police got ready to shoot, she did the only thing that would save my life... she let him have me.

She let this monster take me away.

'You said you'd let me see her again, once you're... done,' I croak after a while. 'You didn't lie, did you?'

'Lie to you, Julie? I'm hurt.' He puts his fist on his heart, like I'm causing him sincere pain. Then his hand slips to my knee. I notice how big his hands are, how many rings he's wearing on each finger. I shift to the other side as far as I can, but my tied legs make it hard to move. His hand keeps resting on my knee, and the Half Face drives the car with the other one, leaning back in his seat and smiling.

'There, can you see it?' he says after another spell of silence. 'We're almost at our destination.'

As he points it out, I watch the sea of lights emerge from the darkness ahead of us. It's like we're approaching a small town, but I know better; I recognize the large tower and the lit-up bridge. This is Fallhallow Airport. So he's actually doing it – he is taking me to a plane, intending us to board it.

I can't believe this is actually happening to me.

My heart begins to beat faster as a new idea hits me. Maybe they're not just letting me go. Maybe they are all out there, waiting for us to arrive, ready to ambush this two-faced criminal when he is not expecting it. Airports are full of security, aren't they? There is no way anyone is letting me board a plane with a lunatic.

He drives onto a parking lot, slamming the front of the car against the curb before he turns off the roar of the engine. The headlights die out at once. I sit up, as well as I can, expecting to be forced out of the car, but he stops me with a tiny jerk of his hand on my knee.

'Now, pumpkin, things might be getting a little crazy out there, so we're going to have a bit of a talk before we get out, okay?'

'How crazy?' I ask, feeling embarrassed that I can't keep my voice from shaking. 'Are they going to shoot at us?'

'Well, they could *try.*' His tongue flicks out and he licks his lips like a lizard. 'I think it would help if you asked them not to shoot. They'll listen to *you*. And remember; asking gets you almost *a*-ny-where.'

'Or I could tell them to shoot only at *you*.'

He leans towards me, trapping me between the back of the seat and the locked door. 'Are you sure you're ready to go down that road again, Juliet?'

No; no, I'm not really that confident. The throbbing pain in my head is a constant reminder of what happens when the Half Face gets displeased with me. Something hot is stinging the corners of my eyes. I don't want him to see me cry; I don't want to give him that victory. Quickly, I turn my face away. 'It's fine. I'll ask them not to shoot.'

'That's my girl. Oh, you look down.' His hand leaves my knee and slips beneath my chin, lifting my head. I'm shocked to find out how close he is. His eyes, so bright in daylight, are nothing but wells of shadows. 'Think of it as an adventure,' he mutters. 'Have you never wanted to see the world, Julie? All the places that aren't advertised in the glossy magazines? Haven't you ever wanted to experience that wild, uncomfortable, *pure* earth that birthed *every*one at one point in history?'

I can't turn away from that stare; it's like looking at a

terrible road accident. 'Why Mongolia?' I ask hoarsely. 'I just don't understand.'

'Well, see, I told you I have a problem.' His thumb begins to move up and down my cheek. 'Now, you – you believe that I'm like this for fun. That I'm doing what I do for kicks-*ah.* You're scared because I'm so unpredictable. You think I will *snap,*' he snaps the fingers of his other hand right before my eyes; I jump and he lets out a laugh. 'Just like that. But I'm not; no, I'm not like that, Jools. There's something inside...here...' The Half Face points at his heart, then at his brow. 'It's *tied* to me, Juliet. I can't expel it from my body like a bad fever.'

I shake my head at him, confused. 'But Mongolia...?'

'Because it ties me up! Like you – you can't move, so you need *me* to cut the ropes before you're free again. That's how it is, Julie. It's just the same.'

I say nothing to this. After a while, he releases my face and unbuckles both our safety belts. He steps out of the car, making his way around it, and opening the door on the passenger's side to lift me out. I lean against the car awkwardly, out of balance from the ties around my ankles. The Half Face squats before me. I hear the familiar click of his knife, and for a moment I'm almost panicking again. But then he simply cuts the rope around my legs. *I should kick him now.*

But he's already up on his feet again, slamming the door shut. It's too late now; I wasted my chance. I'm angry with myself for being so slow.

'There will be a private jet waiting for us, away from the boarding hall,' he tells me conversationally. It's like he's telling me where to find tomatoes at the grocery store. I manage a nod, thinking that there will be another opportunity for me to flee before we actually board that private jet. There *has* to be. I will try to kick him again, or maybe I can push him, or just run really fast. Or the airport security and the military will stop him. It's going to be alright, I just have to be strong a little longer...

It's like the Half Face can read my thoughts just by staring at my face. He brings his head close to mine. This time, I can feel the cold steel of the knife on my cheek, creeping towards my left eye. 'Don't get your hopes up for rescue, Juliet. I will shoot you before you can even blink.'

I blink vigorously, trying not to look at the sharp point of the knife so close to my vision. 'Don't hurt me, please,' I hear myself whisper.

'Just remember our little agreement. If there's trouble, you'll tell them to back off.'

'What if they won't?'

'You better hope they will. Now, let's take a stroll, shall we?'

The knife is replaced by the gun in an instant, then he pulls me away from the car. His arm finds his way around my shoulders, and this time I don't do anything to slip away from him. He guides me towards the brightly-lit building of the airport.

As we get closer, I notice something is off. I have been at Fallhallow Airport before, years ago, when me and my sister were going on our first holiday without Mom. We'd flown to Paris. I remember the airport as a busy place, crowded with people boarding and landing, picking up or dropping off family and friends. Now, the place seems just...dead.

I spot the first police car when we take a sudden turn away from the boarding hall. The Half Face seems to know his way with exact precision, taking me through a smaller alley, which leads directly to a backwater landing ground. The airstrip is lit up brightly, but the area still feels dark to me. There's a plane with the airstairs lowered, ready for anyone to climb aboard.

*No,* I think. *Please, no. Don't let it come that far.*

The police cars are parked on both sides of the plane, their headlights on, though the sirens are turned off.

They're standing there like the military during a salute, just like the officers and the soldiers that rise to greet us when we step into the full light.

I recognize the man with the megaphone. He no longer uses the thing, but simply talks in a clear, loud voice. 'Half Face, we urgently request you to re-open negotiations.'

The Half Face doesn't seem to be listening; he keeps pushing me forward to the plane.

'You do not have to go through with this. Give us Juliet and we will try and accommodate your other wishes as best we can.'

'Yes, I do. I do have to,' he mutters. I doubt anyone but me can hear him.

'You could go alone,' I try, praying that he will not take my words as insolence and hit me again. 'I..I could get you as far as the plane, and then you can board alo –'

'This is *not* a negotiation, Juliet,' he snarls. 'Keep moving.'

I shut my mouth, my mind racing feverishly for something that can still save me, a last-minute rescue plan. Just a few minutes ago, I thought I could kick or push him, but now the cold metal of the gun pressed to my head is reminding me why I shouldn't struggle. We're so close to the plane now. It looks much bigger from up close, though it's still just a small aircraft in comparison to the gigantic airplanes that are used to cross the large oceans of the world. I wonder if it's even big enough to fly all the way to Ulaanbaatar from here.

'Half Face, this is our last warning.' It's not the mediator who speaks now. This man wears a police uniform; he must be the inspector in charge of the team. 'We do not want Juliet on that plane. If you won't surrender the girl, we will commence –'

'NOTHING! YOU WILL COMMENCE TO DO NOTHING!' His roar buckles my knees. If he had not been holding me so tightly, I'm sure I would have sunk to the ground right there. Now his grip on me changes; his right arm coils around my waist, pressing his front into my back in a way that is too close, too intimate. His left arm crosses my chest, the gun openly pointing at the side of my head. 'You only have *one* choice – do you want the girl alive or do you want her dead? You have five seconds. Five.'

I stare at all the policemen who are pointing their firearms at the Half Face. Of course, they're also pointing them at me. Every gun is positioned to fire bullets at *my* body, and I could be left as a bloody pulp if something escalates.

I realize that nobody is going to be able to do a thing. Maybe they're going to try, but the outcome has already been decided: I will end up in that plane, with the Half Face as my captor, or on the ground, with my brains and my blood soiling the airstrip.

Remembering the Half Face's earlier words to me, I somehow find the strength to open my mouth and call: 'Don't shoot! Don't do anything!'

'...Four, three, two...'

'I will go with him!' I shout, desperately. 'I'm gonna go – please don't shoot! Just...just let me go.'

'One –' the Half Face says.

'We're stepping down.' The inspector raises his empty hands in a sign of surrender, slowly taking a step back to his car. The others do the same, lowering their weapons.

The Half Face doesn't waste time talking. He crosses the last few steps to the steps of the plane and pushes me up. I'm immediately surrounded by the cool, dry breeze of air conditioning. The Half Face is close behind me, pushing me all the way to the front of the plane, where I sink down on a random seat.

There's only one other person aboard; a nervous-looking air hostess, whose hands are visibly shaking as she helps me to buckle the safety belt.

'Now, there will be food and drink on board for you, and there are a few movies on the – on the screen ahead of you.' She points at the television screen embedded in the back of the seat in front of me. 'You can find blankets in the luggage compartment and there's a First Aid Kit in the closet over there. Oh, and the bathroom is just ahead of you, and if you feel sick at any time during the flight, you can find the bags beneath your seat...'

'Enough.' The Half Face has turned around and is now glaring at us. 'You're not needed,' he says coldly, waving the gun just once. 'Leave.'

The air hostess hesitates. She reaches out and takes my cold hand in hers, squeezing it in an attempt to reassure me. I can't return the smile she's giving me.

Something hard digs into my palm. My eyes snap up to meet hers, but she is already looking away, giving my captor a final scared look before she lets go of me and turns away, leaving us alone in the narrow tube that is the inside of the airplane.

I don't dare to open my hand. Whatever she has given me is small and square and hard; made of some kind of metallic material. I'm disappointed that it is not a knife, and mystified what else could possibly help me now.

The Half Face doesn't notice my confusion. He drops

into a seat, smiling, and puts away that awful gun. A tiny knot in my belly relaxes. I guess he no longer needs it, now that we've been sealed off from the rest of the world and locked in this small little universe, where he has me all to himself.

And he doesn't need it, because the airplane's door closes. A little while later, the engine starts running, roaring like a monster.

I'm on a plane to Ulaanbaatar, Mongolia. And there's nothing that can stop the Half Face from doing whatever it is he wants with me.

I pull up my legs and curl up in my seat like a frightened kitten. The strange object in my hand does nothing to console me; nothing at all.

# Chapter 6

## Beneath a half-moon

We've been in the air for maybe three hours before I open my hand to look at the object the air hostess slipped into my palm. It looks like a tiny, square coin. I frown down at it. It's like nothing I have ever seen before. It could just be a piece of scrap metal, but then, it looks too polished for that. I turn it around. On the backside is an engraved number, hardly visible as I turn the coin in the artificial light of the plane.

It's not a weapon, unless it could somehow explode. I consider that thought for a second, but it seems too unlikely. Anyway, I have no desire to blow up the plane and myself with it.

*It could be a tracker*, I think. I remember seeing chips as small as these on television; almost invisible objects that trace the location of anything or anyone that carries them along, sending back the coordinates.

My heart lifts. A tracker is just what the police would give me in case they were not able to free me without incident. They know that the Half Face is headed to Mongolia, after all. The plane will ensure that we get as far as Ulaanbaatar, but from there, I have no idea what his plans are. A tracker would at least tell the people back home where I am, at every hour, every minute. It's not the same as having someone to watch over me, but I feel much better now that I know that they are following me.

Now I have to make sure that the Half Face can never find it.

I get up, feeling shaky from the plane's movements, and gently walk forward. The Half Face is sitting a few seats ahead of me, and when I pass him, he reaches out for me with his hand. 'What do you think you're doing?'

'I just have to use the bathroom,' I lie, my eyes trained on the floor.

'Don't take too long.'

What does he imagine I can do in the bathroom that will get him into trouble? I don't ask him, but simply nod and slip past him. The bathroom is just a cubicle with a toilet seat. At least it's clean. I lock the door and lean my back against it.

The most logical place to conceal the chip is the pocket of my skirt. But what if it somehow falls out – what if the Half Face suddenly decides to search me? I remember that he mentioned something about bringing me new, warmer clothes once we arrive.

The crazy idea of swallowing the thing runs through my head. I dismiss it at once; I am terrible with pills, and anyway, the chip would simply leave my body as soon as I had to visit the bathroom for real. I button down my blouse and slip the chip inside my bra, where it feels uncomfortable only for a second.

This is good, I decide. Even if I have to change clothes, I probably won't have to worry about changing my underwear. I take a couple of seconds to breathe deeply, then flush the toilet to make my visit here seem believable.

When I want to go back to my seat, the Half Face stops me. He beckons me over and I reluctantly do what he says, making my way back to where he is still sitting with that relaxed smile on his face.

'Sit with me,' he says, and, when I hesitate: 'Come, you can have the window seat.'

He takes my wrist. I see no other option than to obey, and awkwardly step over his legs to reach the seat on his right. I feel caged, trapped between the window and his muscular frame. To distract myself, I peer through the dirty glass. It's still night out there, but the plane has broken through the clouds and I catch a glimpse of a brilliantly silver crescent moon.

'You look pale.' The Half Face is observing me. I can see him staring at me from the corner of my eye, but I try to ignore it.

'Look at me. Hey.' He takes a hold of my chin and turns my face to him. I passively look back at him. 'Are you scared, Julie?'

I nod.

'Well, there's no need for that. I'm not going to hurt you; not now.'

'You already have hurt me,' I say, making my voice as steady as possible. My head is still aching, and I feel occasional spells of dizziness overtake me. 'You choked me and pushed me and threatened to plant a bullet in my head.'

'Yes,' he says, and I'm stunned to see a flicker of

embarrassment in his eyes. 'But that's all over now. Nobody is threatening *me*, so no one is threatening *you*.'

'They will arrest you as soon as we land,' I say confidently.

'You think so? Maybe you're underestimating how much they want you *alive*. Besides, do you really want to go through all that again, Julie? I know how scared you were. I could feel you trembling all over.'

The thought of him having been so close that he'd felt my body tremble makes an uncomfortable heat rush to my jaws.

'It would be easier if you just went along with me,' he continues, not noticing or not caring about my embarrassment. 'No guns this time, no threats, no shouting. Just you and me. Then I'll take you back home safe and sound. Wouldn't that be better, Julie? Wouldn't it?'

'I don't know,' I mutter. 'Maybe.'

'And yet you still look like I might rip you apart,' he chuckles. He shocks me when he raises a finger and nearly touches my lips. 'I will put a smile on you. Just you wait-ah.'

The plane gives a big shudder and drops a few centimeters, giving me the feeling that I've just jumped off a diving board. The lurch in my belly makes me cough. The Half Face's finger drops and I see him suddenly tighten up.

'Are you scared of flying, Jools?'

'Not really,' I say. 'It's just a little turbulence.'

'Well, I am. And I don't like this. Not. At. All.'

'Then why in *God's name* are we doing this?!' I blurt out, forgetting myself.

He smiles tightly at me. 'Sometimes, fear is the signal telling us that we're on a very important mission.'

I can't think of a single retort, so we wait in silence for the plane to settle down. When it does, he visibly relaxes.

'Now, how about a movie? I like Shrek; don't you?'

'I don't...I don't care.'

He smiles again, and his ringed fingers press a couple of buttons on the screen in front of us. As the movie starts to play, he slides back in his seat, legs outstretched in front of him. His arm falls heavily around my shoulders and he begins to play with my hair, curling it around his fingers.

'Don't,' I say, feeling suddenly cold all over. 'Please.'

'Don't talk during the movie, Juliet.'

I've learned that using my full name means trouble. Still, I ignore the warning in his voice and lean away from him. When that doesn't help, I raise my hand to slap away his.

His hand tightens around my hair and the back of my head explodes in pain. I can't help but let out a whimper.

He doesn't say a word. He just stares at me for a while, those bright blue eyes shadowed by anger, as if he's challenging me to retaliate. It's no use fighting him, I realize. All I get for my efforts is more pain.

After a few frantic heartbeats, he relaxes his hold on me, and I'm able to move my head back to its usual position. I'm going to have to watch out for myself from now on, I decide. At least until somebody saves me.

'Now, let's just watch, Jools,' he says quietly. The storm has left his eyes; he's focusing his attention on the movie again, though his hand remains tangled in my hair. 'Oh, I love the onion-joke!'

Somewhere halfway during the movie, I feel myself getting nauseous. It's getting harder to stay awake; my focus slips away and back, sometimes catching a scene or two, sometimes blanking out completely, leaving me to wonder why time is skipping around in such an erratic manner.

It must be the shock, I catch myself thinking, during one of my brighter moments. Or perhaps I'm not as good with flying as I thought I was. What was the last thing I ate?

My hands are cold. Soon after I discover this, the rest of my body starts to shiver. I only feel a comfortable warmth where the Half Face is keeping his arm around my shoulders.

My head begins to sag, my eyes closing automatically. A new wave of nausea spreads through my belly, worse than before. And God – my head is still throbbing. It's like I can feel the nausea all the way up there.

Without realizing it, I let out a moan.

The Half Face stops twiddling with my hair. I feel the movement of his arm, even if I'm too exhausted to open my eyes and look at him.

'Anything...amiss-*ah*?'

I shake my head, determined not to show my weakness. 'I'm fine,' I whisper, before falling into a claustrophobic darkness.

When I wake up, I'm in one of the double seats, my head propped up by a folded blanket. There's another blanket covering me from my feet to my chin. I don't remember pulling the blankets out, nor do I remember lying down on the seats, but I'm glad that I am no longer supposed to watch the movie.

The shivering seems to have lessened. Still, I feel strangely out of it. The inside of the airplane flutters before my eyes.

'Julie,' the Half Face's voice says. I turn my attention to him as he is bending over me. 'Say your name.'

'What – what do you mean?' Is this one of his games? Is he having an attack of...whatever it is that psychopaths have? 'You know my name.'

'Ah!' He smiles and taps my cheek playfully. 'You're fine.'

He retreats, and I'm left to stare at him for a while, puzzled and wondering what he means. It's not easy to think. Sleep has subdued the pain in my head, but instead I now feel like I have a load of cotton stored in my skull.

When it doesn't seem like he's going to bother me again, I pull the blanket up higher, covering my head as well as my body. The airplane is shuddering and shaking, but that doesn't scare me.

To my own surprise, I slip back into blessed sleep, only to be woken once again. I stare at the Half Face's black-and-white contours.

'Tell me a joke, Julie.'

I close my heavy eyelids, open them again and shake my head. 'Why are you doing this?'

'Good.' He licks his lips and stands up straight. 'It's not funny, but it works. Try to sleep.'

When, after another two hours, I feel his hand shaking my shoulder again, I sit up with difficulty, swaying on the spot, the blanket wrapped around me like a cocoon. 'Why can't I *sleep*? Please just let me rest!'

'I'm looking out for you, Julie,' he says softly. There's a glass in his hand, filled with a strange, thick white liquid. 'Take this.'

I'm immediately alarmed, even in my heavy, dreamlike state. Leaning back as far as I can, I say: 'No! What is it?'

'Paracetamol.' He drops to his knees next to me, forcing the glass to my lips, his other hand snaking to the small of my neck, so that I can't move away again. Feeling trapped, I obediently drink the liquid, swallowing the bitter taste.

'Now, lie back.' He pushes me down before I can argue. His fingers briefly brush over my glowing cheeks, up to my brow. 'Dream sweetly, Juliet.'

'Wait,' I mutter. 'Why am I feeling so bad?'

I think he starts saying something, but the reply is distorted and distant, like he's talking to me from behind a thick plate of glass. I try to focus on his face, hovering so close that I still think I can feel his breath. All I see is the dark of night, lit up by half a moon.

# Chapter 7

## The empty land

Whatever was wrong with me during the flight seems to have disappeared when the airplane finally lands at the Chinggis Khaan International Airport of Mongolia.

I feel like I have been locked up inside this plane forever. As soon as the little green light signals that we have come to a definite stand-still, I'm ready to leap out like any normal passenger.

But of course, we're not normal passengers, and there are still obstacles to be overcome. The Half Face looks tense. He's not pressing his gun to my head – not yet, at least – but he's fidgeting with the holster strapped to his side. I sit in a chair, my legs pressed together, the palms of my hands sweaty. The silence is almost tangible.

Finally, the door at the front of the plane slowly lowers. For the first time I wonder about the pilot who has flown us all the way here. Is he a pilot for the military? Was he scared to be on board with us? He never once made his presence known through the speakers or by coming out of the cockpit. I wish he had; then I wouldn't have felt so abandoned.

I don't get to look around for him, because the Half Face motions for me to come forward to slip his arms around me in that terrifying but familiar way: one arm around my waist, so that I can't move too far away from him, and one arm crossing over my chest, the point of the gun close to my temple.

His breath tickles in my ear. 'This will be over soon.'

I don't answer him; I simply go where he pushes me: down the gangway, into the new, unfamiliar sights and smells of the airport.

There are ten policemen waiting for us. They're standing around the plane in a semicircle, tanned and dark-haired and frowning. *Arrest him now,* I beg them in my mind. I don't care if they jump on him, shoot him in the legs or plunge a dagger into his back, as long as those muscular arms release me.

The Half Face doesn't want to take any chances, it seems. He briefly motions with the gun before it finds its place against my head again. 'Stand in single file,' he orders. 'I don't want anyone *behind* me.'

I wonder if talking English to them is any use, but then all the officers move to form a straight line, and one of them replies: 'We are charged with the protection of your hostage.'

Frustration sweeps over me in such a powerful wave that I can't hold it in. 'You idiots!' I shout. 'Get me away from here!'

The Half Face tenses up. Clearly, he had not been expecting this. 'I will blow her brains onto the pavement,' he growls. 'Stand. Down-*ah!*'

The man who spoke before mutters an order in his own language. The other policemen look uncomfortable. Nobody draws his weapon, and I'm left to stand here all alone, tightly pressed against the monster that will shoot me without a heartbeat of hesitation.

'We are here to escort you to your hotel,' the inspector finally says. 'Do not harm the girl.'

'Don't give me a reason to.'

They walk with us to an old-looking car, the driver

invisible behind a black screen that separates the front of the car from the back seats. The Half Face shoves me inside, quickly following me. Someone closes the door and the car starts moving. I don't understand how the Half Face is allowing himself to be driven off like this. Me, I feel less in control by the second, now that even the Mongolian police seem to decide it is in my better interest to just leave me with a tattooed lunatic.

The car offers very little space for our legs. His knee brushes against mine the entire time. He lets his hand rest on my thigh, the gun in my lap. I stare at it. A part of me wants to reach out and grab it, then shoot him  like he threatened to do to me. My hand is already edging closer to the weapon, my whole body tensing up.

At the last moment, he snaps his hand with the gun away. I flinch, expecting some kind of punishment.. But when I look up, his gaze is fixed on the window. Could it be he hasn't even noticed?

'Look, Jools,' he says, using the gun to point outside.

In order to look where he is pointing, I have to lean over him. I do it reluctantly, mostly because I don't want to give him a reason to hurt me, now that I have just escaped another punishment.

We're driving through the outskirts of the city. I look

at the Soviet-style buildings: grey skyscrapers and rundown houses, the monotone colors occasionally interrupted by brightly painted billboards. The late evening light paints the city faintly orange. The city ends abruptly and unceremoniously. Beyond the last few four-story apartments and what looks like an industrial park behind the freeway, the land suddenly unfolds like a large, green blanket. There are shapes of mountains in the distance, a huge, darkening sky that stresses the wideness of the steppe, and a scattering of white, round tents on the first hill beyond the city's edge. I recall the word that belongs to that image: *gers.*

'That's the empty land,' the Half Face says, shaking me from my reverie. He turns his head to me, smiling, and adds more softly: 'Tomorrow, we'll sail out into that sea.'

The car finally stops at a large, square building with a dirty front. A blue neon sign reads: HOTEL.

Our driver reveals himself as he steps out of the car, opening the door on my side. The Half Face reaches out a hand as if to grab me, but I quickly scoot away from him and let the other man help me out of the car. It is a middle-aged man. He is clean-shaven and his dark face is lined. His eyes bore into mine for a second.

'Thank you,' I mutter.

He doesn't reply; perhaps he can't understand my English.

The Half Face comes to stand beside me. I can see him scrutinizing the surroundings and I know that he is looking for the small police force that greeted us at our arrival. They are not here.

While I feel only disappointment and anger, this discovery seems to lift his spirits. 'The hotel staff won't know *who* we are,' he tells me. 'And *you* will not tell a single soul. Will you, Juliet?'

I give him a dirty look, to which he replies by lifting up the corners of his mouth in that lopsided grin that I have come to loathe.

'Well, pumpkin,' he says. 'Let's check in.'

As we walk to the entrance of the hotel, I'm stopped by a heavy hand that falls on my shoulder. I freeze immediately, but it is just the driver, giving me that same sharp look as before.

'Luggage?' he says, with a heavy accent.

'No – I don't have any.'

For some reason, he shakes his head, so briefly that I can barely see it. 'The chip. You have it?'

I stare at him, too baffled to think of a reply. The Half Face turns around, sees that I'm falling behind, and takes two quick steps back, arriving at my side with a snarl on his face. The driver is forced to let me go as the Half Face locks his fingers around my wrist and pulls me along.

My head is reeling with new hope. Perhaps this is the reason that the Mongolian police force did not try to arrest him during our landing, or during our transportation through the city. They might actually have a plan to rescue me. Of course they aren't going to do anything that could escalate the already tense situation. It makes sense, I think, my heart pounding excitedly. Thinking about the chip makes me conscious of the tiny, metallic coin inside my bra, safely hidden. Knowing that my captor is not aware of this secret makes me feel a little better.

This small resurgence of optimism is quickly dampened when we are shown to our hotel room. It's a narrow chamber, with a rickety desk in one corner, a dusty window looking out over the street, the door to what I assume is the bathroom in the other corner, and two single beds in the middle, pushed together to create a king-size bed. I notice the double comforters. That's some relief, at least, though it's not much.

I turn to the Half Face, a pleading look in my eyes. 'Couldn't I have my own room?'

He chuckles. 'Then how will I know you won't *slip out* at night, Julie?'

I hadn't even thought of that. I walk over to the window, staring down. Not a sign of the black car that drove us here, nor of its driver. I feel a tiny jab in my stomach – for the briefest of moments, I had felt like I was with an ally. Another part of me is relieved; this way, the Half Face won't notice anything suspicious.

I feel the warmth of his body as he comes to stand behind me, his hands on my shoulders. He squeezes my muscles gently, resting his chin on the top of my head. 'It's not beautiful, but it *is* intriguing.'

It takes me a moment to realize that he is talking about the part of the city that we're looking at. Here, too, the view is dominated by square blocks with rows of windows, shabby walls and peeling paint. It's like the city of Ulaanbaatar has been left to slowly collapse in on itself after the Soviet Union unraveled and the Russians left.

When I don't say anything, he leans in even closer. 'What's the matter, birdy? Cat got your tongue-*ah*?'

I consider making a snarky reply, but I just don't have the heart. My arms are still bruised from where he grabbed me two days ago...God, has it only been two days? I close my eyes, suddenly beyond exhausted.

'Julie, Julie, *Julie*,' the Half Face sighs, his breath brushing my neck, warm against my cheek. 'You've come this far with me already. Why don't you just enjoy the ride?'

He adjusts his head. Before I realize what he is planning, his lips gently brush my skin. He kisses my neck, just long enough to make all my hairs stand up.

Even after all he's done, this comes as a surprise. I'm too shocked to move. He apparently takes my lack of response as encouragement, because his arm slides from my shoulder, over my back and under my arm to my belly. 'I thought you were beautiful when you walked into that court room,' he murmurs. 'So determined. So *nervous*.'

I try to think of a reply – anything at all – but when he tries to kiss me again, I simply lean away. 'Stop. I'm not your girlfriend.'

'Oh, Juliet!' he chuckles. 'I know exactly what you are.'

'Yes – I'm your prisoner.'

'And my companion.' He runs his fingers through my hair, sending an involuntary shiver down my spine. 'And I lov –'

'No!' I spin on my heels and duck to get away from the window, and his arms. 'Don't say it! Don't even think it! It's wrong and...and insane, and you don't *know* me!'

'Juliet –'

'No!' I shout again, my voice rising. 'I – I need to be alone. Just leave me the hell alone!'

He looks so perplexed that, for a moment, I think he will really let me get away with my attitude. Then his hand shoots forward like an attacking snake, and he grabs my shoulders so hard that I feel a bruise forming immediately. Still, I stare at him, tears of anger and pain in my eyes.

I manage to choke out, 'You're *terrible.*'

He tightens his grip, shoving  my head against the wall.  I'm immediately engulfed by waves of nausea and dizziness,  but he catches me before I fall.

'Doesn't make a difference if you hurt me,' I wheeze, when I finally have enough air again. 'Just – makes you *worse!*'

I fully expect more punishment, and shut my eyes tightly in fearful anticipation. When it doesn't come, I look up at him. His hands come up to cup both sides of my  face. The Half Face stares at me with eyes that burn as sparks in the darkness. His mouth is a tight line, his eyebrows deeply creased; his anger is palpable – and yet, he doesn't strike again. I'm starting to feel like he is angry at something else.

Using this brief, confusing moment of intermission to

its full advantage, I slink away from him, to the only escape route that I can think of: the bathroom. I lock the door as soon as I'm in, feeling that the tiny 'click' of the door lock is the most soothing sound I've heard in days, and sink to the floor with my back to the white tiled wall.

'Juliet, don't lock yourself in there!'

I ignore the Half Face's command. The bathroom is small, but at least it's clean. There's a glass shower cell, a white sink with a mirror and a towel rack with four equally white towels, neatly folded. I'm relieved to discover small tubes of toothpaste and shampoo on one of the shelves of a small closet below the sink. There are even some toothbrushes, still in their plastic wrappers. I haven't brushed my teeth since before the hearing.

'Julie, just open the door for me.'

I remain where I am, even holding my breath. He can't crash through the door with the lock turned, can he? No – he wouldn't. It would draw too much attention if he had to explain why our door is broken, and attention is exactly what he doesn't want. Even so, my heart keeps hammering until he grows silent again.

How long I stay there, sitting on the floor next to the sink, I don't know. Eventually I grow cold. I inspect my upper arms, where he grabbed me, and find two matching angry, red bruises. When I look in the mirror, I see the purple bruises from when he grabbed my windpipe. I rinse my mouth and splash some water on my face, then stare up at my reflection once more.

I look ragged. My hair falls over my shoulders in dull tresses, the curls messy and unkempt. There are dark circles under my eyes – not because of the Half Face, but because I'm just so exhausted.

My skin, when I touch my hands to my face, is icy cold. I take a towel and wrap it around myself, but the cloth doesn't keep the cold out much. What do I do now? I'm too afraid to leave the bathroom, but I'm too cold and too sore to wait in here much longer.

Perhaps I should just take a shower.

The idea of undressing when the Half Face is just in the other room appalls me, even if the door is locked. He will hear the water running, and then he will know... Perhaps he'll even imagine me naked, thinking about running his lips over my neck again, and then he might...

I stop myself at once, forcing the thought from my head.

I'll have to wash myself *sometime*. Now might be the only chance I get. I breathe in deeply, then turn on the hot water of the shower. As the steam fills the narrow glass cubicle, I slowly, painfully, undress. My blouse and skirt fall on the ground; for a moment, I stare at them. I picked them only for the hearing. I had wanted to look neat, grown-up, in control. Now I wish I had gone with a pair of sturdy jeans and a blazer.

My body hurts when I step into the shower. I close my eyes, concentrating on the sensation of the hot water spilling over my body, quickly suppressing the shivers that have been running through me since the Half Face put his mouth to my skin. After a while, my muscles begin to relax, and the aching feeling in my head stops. I grab a tube of shampoo and rub my hair vigorously, then unpack one of the toothbrushes and brush my teeth for at least five minutes.

Just the act of cleaning up makes me feel a bit better.

When my skin begins to get wrinkly, I finally turn off the water, and I wrap myself in the soft towels. My clothes don't smell so fresh when I put them back on, but since I have no luggage, there's nothing else for me to wear. I run my fingers through the wet tresses of my hair, brushing it as best I can.

I catch another glimpse of myself in the mirror. I still look tired, but now my skin is blushing from the warm water.

I realize that I can no longer avoid my confrontation with the Half Face, unless I'm willing to spend the night in here.

I'm not.

With nervous hands, I first unlock the door of the bathroom. I wait. Nothing happens, which means he's not standing on the other side, ready to burst in. Gingerly, I open the door, glancing through the crack. He's sitting in the only chair that is present in the room, next to the rickety desk in the corner. There are a few plastic bags on the desk, and the smell of take-out food drifts my way. My stomach gives a big lurch; suddenly, I realize how hungry I really am. I had a little of the airplane food, but I had been too scared and then too ill to really eat much. Take-out seems incredibly good right now.

At the sound of the door creaking, the Half Face turns his head to me. His eyes run over my body, from the creased skirt to my wet hair. He doesn't get up. 'Have you calmed down?'

I nod, deciding that I will not speak to him, unless I absolutely cannot avoid it.

He takes one of the plastic bags and holds it out to me. 'It's still hot. Eat it quick.'

I take it and move to the bed furthest away from him.

Inside the bag is a burger, a cardboard box with fries and something that tastes like chicken. Now is not the time to tell him that I've been a vegetarian for over a year. I hungrily devour my meal, ignoring the silence that has fallen between us. When I am done, he takes the empty bags from me and throws a bundle of clothes next to me.

'Put these on. You'll be warmer.'

I examine the clothes. There's a blue long-sleeved T-shirt, a soft, warm sweater in the same color and another hooded fleece jacket. There is also a pair of pants; not the pair of jeans I was thinking about, but a brown, well-insulated pair that looks like it will fit me so perfectly that it's almost scary. How did he know my size? Could he guess just by looking at me?

'There're hiking boots and a water-proof jacket in the backpack, but you don't need those now,' he says. 'I advise you to sleep early, Juliet. Long day, tomorrow.' He smiles.

So he's no longer angry. I feel relieved, though not much more at ease.

Silently, I take off my shoes, placing them neatly on the ground next to the bed. I feel his stare even without looking up.

'Come on,' he grins now. 'You can take off more than that.'

I shake my head, slip under the comforter and pull it around me as tightly as I can. I hear him chuckle, before he goes and turns off the lights. Suddenly, the room is bathed in darkness.

A moment later, he settles next to me, facing my back. He moves his arm, putting it around me, though the thick comforter separates him from my actual body.

I stiffen, and consider moving back to the bathroom. But then what? I'll be less cold and more comfortable here, and the Half Face is going to sleep anyway, and he's going to use this bed, so I might as well stay and try to make the best of it. As long as we're on this journey together, there will be no escaping him.

I hold my tongue when his hand moves to my head and starts to brush through my hair, moving slowly, as though he expects me to fall asleep by his touch. I still hold my tongue when, after a while, he starts to speak. His voice drifts through the darkness.

'So when I was a kid, I was a middle child. My daddy was a real professor, always reading, always very *smart*. And my mom, you know, she used to tell me how I was the handsomest boy of my class, and how I was clever, like my dad. But one day, she...got...hit-*ah*. By a bus. Never even saw the other side of the street. And now, you see, we were devastated, because my father knew a lot about anthropology but not a lot about raising kids. And then he brought home all sorts of things – rum, whiskey, bourbon. Classy, at first, you would think, Julie, but not for very long. And we discovered how our smart daddy was a harsh daddy, when he got drunk. Julie, turn around.'

I don't immediately respond, but he tugs at my shoulder, until I feel that I had better just do what he tells me before I end up with another bruise. I shift to my other side, so that I'm facing him.

'So, very soon, the alcohol wasn't the only thing he brought home to us, Julie. He had five drinking buddies, all middle-aged men, who liked to brawl and hit things and look at my sister funny. One night, ah...somebody slapped her. Right-in-the-face. Like this.' He mimics a fist-punch to my jaw, causing me to flinch. He swallows audibly. 'So I stand up and I *kick* him. I kick him hard; I kick him *so* hard that his balls are bleeding. He didn't... like... that. Another one grabbed my arms and pushed me down on my knees. And I was only ten years old, Julie. Can you imagine what it feels like to be pushed on your knees-*ah*...by a grown man, while your daddy is watching?

'When he was all finished he took his cigarette,' the Half Face holds up his hand as if he's holding an invisible cigarette himself, then presses his finger into my cheek, 'and he marked me. Here, and *here.* Then all the way up here.' His finger trails from my chin to just below my eye. Instinctively, I flinch and turn my face away.

'I tried that too,' he says. 'But the others, they just grabbed me and held...me...still. And then it was too late, you see; my face was already *burning.* You can feel it if you want...Come here. Hey. It's okay, just your hand.' He grabs my hand and guides it to his face. And yes, now I notice the rough patches of scar tissue on his skin; in the corner of his mouth, on the line of his jaw and up to his cheekbone. The stark contrast of black and white ink conceals the ugly burn marks to the eye, but not to my shaking fingers.

''Course, we couldn't stay after that. My sister said we had to go. *But go where?* I asked. She didn't know, but she was scared. So she told me to return home after school the next day, just to pick up some things, while she took my little baby brother and never went home. This way, we were less suspicious to my dad, see? She told me to wait, said she'd come back when she had found a place to stay. And I did what she told me; I went home. And that evening, daddy invites his buddies – as usual – and they drink *more* than usual. Then one of them discovers his books. And he says, *what is this?* And my daddy, he tells them a-a-all about the tribes in Africa and their spirit workers, and their superstitions and everything he remembers before he passes out. And the others, they laugh and they guffaw and they think he is mighty funny. So they take a spell out of the book, and they chant, and roar, and chant some more, and they tell me that they're summoning a spirit. Just for me. I run... out of the room, but they catch me anyway, and lock me up. In my own closet. Where it's dark and cramped. And I'm scared of the dark, Julie. I get even more scared when they leave me there and make funny voices, and bang on the door to frighten me. So I sit there, and I cry. And I beg. And I *yell-ah.* Nobody comes; no-bo-dy cares. But *some*thing moves in the darkness next to me, and I can't guess what it is...until it talks.'

'What?' I interrupt, too baffled to remember that I had decided to be silent.

'It whispered to me, Julie, like a little voice in my head. It told me its name was Black, and he had listened to the spell from the book. You don't believe me. You're making a face like I'm a *cra-zy* person.' I hear him lick his lips, and he brings his face closer to me, breathing hard. 'It's true, Juliet. He came inside me like fever, but he helped me escape. And when I found my sister at last, she wept and wept for my face. That night, I had a dream – I dreamed that my mother was weeping and weeping, just like sis. She said how disfigured I had become, how it hurt her eyes to see me now. I woke up *angrier* than before. I stayed angry for months. Can you imagine that, Julie? Months of anger? How it *consumes* you?

'So one day, I wrapped my hands around the throat of my little baby brother. He choked and cried, and my sister had to hit me on the *head* before I let go. I left, of course. Never came back.'

'You *killed* your brother?' I'm barely able to whisper, that's how sick I suddenly feel.

'No, no, Juliet. But I *could have.* You think I was *proud* of what I'd done? Hm? Y'think I didn't feel soiled to the depth of my soul?'

'I..I don't know,' I reply, still quietly. I recall the shooting at Fallhallow National Bank; how can he feel ashamed about his behavior, yet continue to destroy other lives in the spur of a moment?

'Well, I searched for a way to appease the Black,' he continues, as though he hadn't heard me. 'Yet at the same time, I grew strong on his anger. This malice of his. It helped me survive. And in time, he got...embedded...in me.

His hunger turned into mine. His cravings: mine. And so I did this.' He points at his face again, and I understand he means the large tattoo. 'To remember what I was, and to whom I owed it. Up until...now.'

When the silence stretches, I understand that his story is finished. Slowly, I shake my head. 'Why has it changed now?'

He brings his head even closer, mouth pressed to my ear, as if he wants to share a secret that cannot even reach the door of this room. 'I want to *expel* it.'

'Why?'

'Isn't it *obvious*? I want to be free. That's why we're here, Julie. You'll see. You'll see tomorrow.'

# Chapter 8

## Company

I'm roused from a restless sleep by the Half Face, who is pacing through the room. He shoves a bag of cold leftovers from the night before towards me as a breakfast, then leaves the room without so much as locking the door. I stare after him. Is this a trick?

I scramble off the bed. My stomach is growling, but I can't decide if I should spend my time eating and building up my strength, or by grabbing this chance to make a run for it.

Maybe he's behind the door, waiting for me to get out. I can't think of a single reason why he would do that, but if

I hadn't already thought it, last night's story made it painfully clear that this man is not right in the head. He could do anything. And I've already learned that most of the things that he does to me *hurt*.

I sit on the bed tensely, eating cold fries and waiting for something to happen. Nothing does, not even when I'm done eating and have wiped my hands on the bed sheets.

I stand up, open the door and glance outside. This corridor of the hotel is deserted. My heart starts hammering like a racehorse. Could I – could I simply walk away right now? As I slip out of the room and walk down to the end of the corridor, my mind starts whirring frantically. I need to make a plan, a real plan, before I get out of this hotel. Where should I go? How will I get there? I don't even speak the language. Surely *someone* will understand the word 'police station'?

Breathing hard, I see a staircase ahead of me, and I start running, my footsteps muffled by the thick, dirty carpet that once must have been red. As soon as I round a corner, I crash into a hard body, forcing me to stop at once. The impact throws me back.

It's the Half Face, looking down on me with an unreadable expression. Before I can react, he grabs both my wrists in his hands and hauls me up to stand in front of him.

'Where do you think you're going?'

I open my mouth, but can't think of anything. What am I going to say: I was looking for you? There's a fire up in our room? There's no real excuse that this guy is going to believe anyway, so I just stare up at him, panting from the run.

'Don't make me hurt you, Jools,' he says quietly. 'Just stop fighting me.'

*I want to go HOME!* I almost shout at him, but his fingers, digging into my wrists, warn me not to get loud. Instead of digging my hole even deeper, I take a step back, lowering my arms to show him that I'm ready to give up my defenses.

'Good girl.'

'Where did you go?' I ask, changing the subject.

'I'll show ya. Come.' Now he's leading me down the same staircase he just emerged from. 'Our ride's here.'

'Ride?'

He doesn't answer, but keeps walking, crossing the lobby, until we reach the entrance of the hotel. Outside on the street is a green van waiting for us. Two men, both clearly native Mongolians, are leaning against the car with tense expressions on their faces.

'Our company, for the rest of the journey,' the Half Face says, making something of a formal bow in their direction.

'I thought we'd be alone.' I'm not sure how I feel about this sudden change. The Half Face scares me, but he is just one man to keep off of me at night. If these guys are anything like him... I try not to think about the worst possibilities.

'Wasn't sure whether they'd obey all my orders,' he grins. 'Did I mention that I have an *excellent* attorney?'

I nod silently. The youngest of the men steps forward and extends his hand to me. He must be around forty. He has deep-set eyes and a receding hairline, and a firmly set jaw. In a heavy accent, he says: 'My name is Batzorig, your interpreter during this trip. You must be Juliet.'

I decide to shake his hand, and I'm surprised by how strong and warm his grip is. 'Yes...that's me.'

'You look tired.'

I'm not sure how to respond to this forward remark.

'My job is also to look after you.'

'That was *not* in the description-*ah!*' the Half Face snaps. He breaks up the handshake by pulling me away from Batzorig, towards himself, causing me to crash into his body for the second time that day.

The interpreter watches the Half Face with a composed face. For a moment, I wonder if I misunderstood him and that he is not aware of the situation, because why else would he look so undisturbed? 'I am a father myself,' he says then. 'It brings the urge to defend. You will understand.'

'Juliet doesn't need defense.'

I swallow, keeping myself from saying something that might get me in trouble.

'This is your driver, Enkhbad,' Batzorig continues, motioning to the other man. 'Also your cook. He speaks little English,' he adds, when he notices the Half Face's suspicious expression. 'I have been briefed by the police, but my orders are explicitly to not interfere. Enkhbad knows nothing.'

Almost as if to demonstrate, the driver grins and points at me. 'Honeymoon, yes?'

I open my mouth, speechless.

'You and him,' he indicates my captor. 'Husband, wife.'

'*Husband?*' I repeat, shocked to the bone. But the Half Face grins and puts his arm around my shoulder in a mockingly loving gesture.

Batzorig starts to say something in rapid Mongolian, but the Half Face holds up his hand. 'Don't correct him,' he tells him, with a hint of relish in his voice. 'The less he knows...well. It lessens the urge to *harm*. You will understand-*ah*.'

Something flashes over the interpreter's face that I can't quite determine. Fear, anger? After a second, it's gone, and he nods curtly.

'We-e-ell,' the Half Face says, letting me go to clap his hands. 'I think we should be off, don't you? Julie? Are you excited?'

'I'm scared.'

'Aw, now, don't be. It's just a little ride.'

We all walk towards the van; Enkhbad climbs behind the wheel, the Half Face glides in one of the spacious backseats and I'm about to follow him when Batzorig halts me with a brief touch to my arm.

'Has he hurt you?' he asks, quietly enough not to be heard inside the van. 'You can tell me.'

'No,' I begin, then pause. What's the point in lying? 'Yes,' I admit therefore, swallowing audibly. 'Sometimes.'

'I noticed your bruises.'

'It's nothing too bad.'

'Did he do – other things?' He must realize what an awkward question this is, because he quickly adds: 'You don't have to tell me details, Juliet. I'm here to look out for you.'

'Juliet!' the Half Face's voice rings out from inside the van. I've come to recognize a command when I hear one. He is losing his patience.

'What's the point?' I ask Batzorig. 'There's nothing you can do for me as long as we're out here. Don't make him angry, that's all there is to try. There's no pleading with him or befriending him.'

'Well, you have one friend now.'

I smile at him before I climb into the car. The Half Face pulls me towards him, to make me sit on the seat next to him. The interpreter is the last to get in, pulling the door shut behind him. The engine starts running, and before I have time to look back at the hotel, Enkhbad drives the van around a corner, heading for the clearly visible edge of the city.

'Say goodbye to Ulaanbaatar,' Batzorig says drily. 'And welcome to the real Mongolia.'

As soon as we leave the big city behind, the scenery changes drastically. I lean to the window of the van, staring – in spite of my predicament – with a growing sense of awe at the vast, open plains that stretch out as far as I can see. The white, round tents that I had seen earlier turn out to be much bigger when we drive past them. They could house a large family and allow them to live spaciously, I think.

'They're called *gers*,' Batzorig says, catching my stare.

'I know.'

'I grew up in one of those,' he says casually, when we pass another clutter of gers on the next hill. 'Never set one foot inside the big city before I was fifteen years old.'

I try to imagine what it would be like to live a life somewhere in this barren steppe, where the lights and the sounds of a city are far away.

'I don't even know what I'd do without my phone,' I admit. Then I realize that I still have it on me; I automatically put it in one of my pockets when I had to change my clothes. I pull it out and watch the screen light up. Of course, there's no reception.

'Give that to me.' The Half Face holds out his hand.

'Why?'

'So I can make a pic-ture. Of you.'

'I don't need a...' Upon seeing his expression, I falter. Really, it's much easier to give him what he wants. My phone is useless to me now. I hold it out to him and he takes it with a hungry expression, like I've just given him the tool to teach him my innermost secrets.

After a moment, he holds the phone up like a camera and says: 'Smile for me.'

I look into the camera but I don't smile. He takes the picture anyway and bends over to show it to me. I look tired and annoyed, hugging my warm new coat in the considerable colder Mongolian air.

'Well, it's still sweet,' he comments, looking at the photo from different angles. 'We'll try a retake some other time.'

I ponder the word 'sweet' coming from such a hardened criminal and look out of the window again. We're following an asphalt road that winds its way through the landscape like a black river. The horizon is dominated by distant mountains, which almost look like clouds from here. We pass a couple of men on horses. Their clothes are a splash of color in the greens and grays of the steppe: bright red, sky blue, sunshine yellow.

'Now that is the only right way to travel around here.' Batzorig points at the horses. 'A car can only get you so far.'

'What are we going to do, then?' I ask.

'There'll be horses waiting for us later on. You're not afraid to ride?'

'Oh, well...I don't think so.'

'Come on, Julie; a girl like you? Never had a fondness for ponies?' the Half Face chuckles.

I shrug. 'Lessons were really expensive.'

'A good horse is not a luxury for these folks, Julie,' he says, surprising me. 'I bet our friend here can testify to that. Isn't that so, Batso – Batman – *ah...*Batzy?'

I nervously glance at the interpreter, to see what his reaction will be. The man clenches his jaw even tighter, but when he replies, it is in a normal voice. 'That's true. Most children learn to ride before they learn to walk.'

'Did you?'

'Oh, yes.' When he smiles at me, it gives his face a genuinely warm expression. 'When I grew up, I had a horse called Ghengis. It won me many races during the Naadam festival. It's too bad you're not here for Naadam. I've even been called *tumny ekh* once, in the Daaga races. Leader of ten thousand.'

'Daaga?'

'It's the two-year-old horse races,' he explains. 'The horses are two years old, of course; not the children. They are usually already five years old.'

I raise my eyebrows.

'Of course, next year, I finished last. They called my Ghengis *bayan khodood.* It means Full Stomach.'

The driver, Enkhbad, turns his head as he steers the van over the empty road. 'Horse eat many much,' he says with a broad grin. 'Fatty horse not run.'

For the first time since my capture, I laugh.

# Chapter 9

## The right diagnosis

We drive for maybe two hours, the van crossing a countryside that constantly changes yet seems to stay the same. Batzorig distracts me by telling me funny anecdotes about his childhood in a traditional Mongolian family; he tells me how his name was chosen by a lama in a Buddhist temple, how his brothers are called Not This One and Not That One, a custom that apparently is so normal in this land that it doesn't raise a single eyebrow.

'It is a simple way of diverting ill-meaning spirits,' he explains to me. As soon as he says it, I'm forced to remember the Half Face's story, and I feel uncomfortable again.

Eventually, Enkhbad turns the car off the road and stops.

'We will need to walk from here,' Batzorig says. 'The camp is not near the road. Juliet, how are your shoes?'

'They're fine,' I say. At least the Half Face has made sure that I have everything I need: my sturdy new clothes shelter me from the sharp, cold gusts of wind that have constant, free reign in this open grassland, and my hiking boots are water-proof and comfortable.

Batzorig opens the back door of the van for me and helps me to jump out, catching me by the arm. I'm grateful for his presence, and for his kindness, but I'm also worried about what the Half Face will do if he decides that the interpreter is getting too chummy with me. I glance at him to see what he's thinking, but to my surprise, his attention seems to be elsewhere. He is gazing ahead of us, his brow creased. For once, there's no grin on that face of his.

'Is it that way?' he asks, not bothering to change the direction of his glance to address our interpreter.

'Yes,' Batzorig says. 'Just a few kilometers into the hills. She is expecting us.'

'She?' Now the Half Face turns around, licking his lip with a little relish. 'That is news to me.'

'Yes, she is a woman.'

We start walking. I feel aimless, having no idea where we're headed or what to expect once we get there. At first, I stay next to the Half Face because he catches me by the arm and pulls me along every time I fall back, but after a while his attention seems to be drawn away from me again, and I quietly fall into step next to Batzorig, walking a little way behind my captor. Enkhbad closes the rear. He is the only one that doesn't look troubled.

'Where *are* we going?' I ask.

Batzorig looks down on me in surprise. 'You don't know?'

'No. He hasn't told me a thing.'

'That's not true, Julie,' the Half Face interjects. He doesn't even look over his shoulder. 'I have told ya everything-*ah*.'

'I guess I'm just too stupid to understand, then,' I mutter rebelliously.

'We are going to see an *idugan*,' Batzorig tells me quietly. 'She is a woman of spirits.'

'A magician?'

'No, there is no magic other than that of spirits. You would call her a shaman.'

'What does she do?'

'Many things. An *idugan* is a healer, a caster of auguries. The *idugan* is our bridge-woman, between our land and the next. She hears the spirits talk and she can bring them to rest.'

With a sudden, clear shock, I think I understand what the Half Face is going to do. 'Can she expel evil spirits?' I ask.

'Yes, perhaps. Sometimes it is...' Batzorig seems to be searching for the right way to explain it. 'Not all spirits are individuals. It can be complicated.'

'So, that's it?' I ask the Half Face, who is still in front of me. 'This is why you have brought me out here? To find a shaman who can cast out Black?'

'Yes.'

I am so amazed that I forget to feel scared. 'So, how is that going to happen?'

'I don't know.'

I look at Batzorig, but he shrugs. 'Shamans have many methods. Not one way is the same.'

Another thought hits me and I direct my question at my captor again. 'Are you frightened?'

The Half Face slows his steps and turns to look at me. There's a strained smile on his lips. 'You'd enjoy that, wouldn't ya, Julie?'

Well, that depends, I think. If he got so scared that he'd take out his worries on me, I think I'd prefer him to be as fearless as he appeared back when he had the firearms of the Fallhallow Police Force aimed at him.

'I am...aah...*anx*ious. I want the right diagnosis at last.'

Right. Because pills and therapy are obviously not the right answer to his problems. 'I don't really believe in spirits,' I challenge him.

'Humanity did not believe the earth is round, yet that is true.'

I turn to Batzorig. 'What about you?'

'Well.' He looks slightly uncomfortable. 'This is part of my native religion, Juliet. But the Soviets did not allow many shamans to keep practicing their old ways. They have been almost driven to extinction.'

'But do you really believe that we can have spirits inside of us?' I ask. I point at our driver and cook. 'Does *he?*'

Batzorig translates my question into Mongolian. Enkhbad doesn't need time to think; he begins to talk at once, his hands moving rapidly up and down.

Batzorig gives a small smile. 'He says he has seen many things that were caused by the interference of ancestors and other spirits. There is no doubt in his mind about their existence.'

'Julie is like a skeptic teetering on the edge of belief,' the Half Face says, patting me on the head, as if I'm a child that has just said something funny. 'She still needs to come to full conversion.'

I don't reply to this. Instead, I retreat inside myself, allowing my thoughts to crash and wash over me like waves of the ocean. Images play out before my mind's eye, things that look familiar, though I have never seen them before. It takes a while before I realize that it's *his* story that I'm imagining: a little boy locked in a closet, so scared that he can feel his heart racing in his throat, almost ready to explode, while cruel men rap on the wardrobe's door, shouting profanities and hissing disturbing things through the thin barrier of wood. The boy huddles up in the darkness, breathing hard, sobbing hysterically into his own arms. It's not hard to conceive how a child's imagination could drive him to some sort of torturous madness.

When I look up, it's harder to imagine that the scarred little boy has transformed into this hardened man; a criminal who doesn't flinch as he pulls the trigger of a gun. A man who has covered himself from head to toe in black ink: spirals and interlocking shapes on his arms, neck, and hands, a white moon and a black shadow on his face.

For the first time I wonder how old he really is. The tattoos make him seem like an almost ageless creature; a nightmare come to life. But he cannot be that old, I reason, as I secretly observe him. Though his voice is low and raw, and the ink on his face hides his scars as well as his age, his eyes are so shockingly bright that I don't think he can be older than thirty.

When he turns his head around and locks eyes with me, as if he can sense me watching him, I shock myself by thinking that he is striking – and almost beautiful – in the way that he moves his body, the manner in which his eyes stand out. He possesses a kind of grace that stems from the symmetry of his face; yin and yang in a perfect balancing act.

I quickly turn my eyes away from him, remembering the many bumps and bruises I have. Predators may be beautiful, but they still have a deadly touch.

Batzorig saves me from my thoughts when he points to a hill ahead and says: 'Over there; it's the campsite.'

I look up, and see that he's right. There's a big, white *ger*; the top visibly peeping over the top of the hill, and when we get closer, I notice a couple of small horses huddling together in a makeshift paddock. There is no sign of people, until Batzorig calls out in Mongolian.

From the *ger* emerges a tiny, ancient woman, dressed in a plain, dark blue tunic that reaches all the way to the ground, tied together at the waist by a red sash. Her dark head is covered by an equally dark hat, pointing upwards. Her face is as wrinkled and lined as old tree bark. Behind her is another woman, clearly younger, though her face, too, is lined.

Though the old woman focuses her attention on the Half Face, the gaze of the younger one skips immediately to me. She asks a question and Batzorig gives a reply, but he doesn't bother to translate.

The old woman mutters something, pointing at the Half Face and then at the rest of our odd little party. This time, Batzorig renders the speech into English.

'She welcomes us all to her home. She says her name is Oyun. Her daughter is called Tsend.'

Oyun says something else, her face furrowed. Batzorig hesitates, then turns to the Half Face. 'She says you are screaming. She heard you screaming from behind the last hill.'

For the first time ever I catch him with a deeply unsettled look on his face.

The youngest of the women, Tsend, steps forward and takes my face between her hands. She says something in a sing-songy voice. Then she shocks me by placing her lips on my forehead, kissing me like I'm a long-lost friend.

I have no idea how to react to this, so I give her an awkward smile and gingerly move a step back. 'What... what did she say?'

'She says...It is hard to translate.' Batzorig ruffles his mop of jet black hair with his hand while he thinks. 'She calls you *judge* and *sojourner*. There's conflict inside of you.'

'I don't think I'm conflicted,' I mutter. Batzorig glances at me with sympathy, and he doesn't translate my words back for Tsend to hear.

The two women usher us inside. There are thick furs on the ground, keeping out the chill and the drought, and two wooden poles in the middle to keep the tent upright; a small stove between them. There are two beds on the other side, covered in brightly dyed rugs. The *ger* is big enough for all of us to sit on the furs and rugs quite comfortably, and I'm surprised at how nice it is in here. Batzorig points out a bench in the other corner, decorated with things that I can't immediately identify.

'That is a shrine to the spirits,' he says.

'Is Tsend a shaman too?'

The woman, who looks up at the sound of her name, begins to talk rapidly. Like Enkhbad, she uses her hands almost as much as her mouth.

'Tsend says that she was seven years old when she was captured by seizures that made her fall to the ground. She was ill for three days, before her grandmother dressed her in her own robes and performed many rituals to bring her back healthy. After that, she could travel to the other world.'

'What *other* world?'

Batzorig shakes his head. 'I know no other word for it.'

'But how does she travel?'

Batzorig translates my question. Tsend smiles again, pointing in the direction of the spirit shrine.

'She says her drum is her most important aid. A drum is like a horse. When you have learned how to ride, it will take you anywhere. You will see what she means soon.'

While I'm mystified, I am also content to sit with my legs crossed on one of the soft furs, soaking up the heat that emanates from the stove. The presence of other women is reassuring, even if I can't directly communicate with them.

When we are all settled, Oyun takes the word for the first time in minutes. Batzorig translates.

'She asks what you have come to find with her.'

'I need to expel an evil spirit,' the Half Face says, with no trace of embarrassment.

'She asks: how do you know that there is evil inside of you?'

The Half Face leans forward, his elbows resting on his crossed legs. 'Because it has burdened me since the day it entered my mind-*ah*. I am not free.'

Oyun nods, as if she's not surprised to hear him say that at all. She says something to her daughter, who replies in soft words, pointing a finger from me to my captor.

'Oyun says that she will have to investigate first.'

'*Investigate*?' the Half Face repeats.

'That is not the word she used. She means...To develop a feeling. She will reach out and explore the energy. Gently,' he adds after Oyun says something else. 'It will be gentle at first.'

Tsend pours water into a small black kettle and puts it on the stove. I shift on my fur. 'Is it possible to go...visit a bathroom?' I ask, not even sure if there is such a place out here. 'I really need to go.'

'Oh.' Batzorig quickly renders my question into Mongolian. Tsend nods, beckoning me outside. I follow her, aware that the Half Face's eyes trail me all the way out.

The woman leads me around the *ger* and the paddock, where a small wooden shed has been built, leaning against the slope of the hill. She points at it.

'Thank you,' I mutter.

There's no toilet inside, just a hole, dug in the earth. The door of the shed covers the doorway only partially, leaving a big part of the ger and the paddock visible. I try to ignore it and squat down.

*This is the weirdest thing I have done in my entire life*, I think. Somehow, my fear has gone; perhaps doused by the presence of other, friendly people; perhaps simply numbed by all the strange, exhausting, new impressions that I'm forced to process.

When I emerge from the shed, I want to snap a picture of the ger and its surroundings. I look for my phone, until I realize that the Half Face still has it.

Oyun pours us all a hot, darkly colored drink after I get back into the tent.

'What is it?' I ask.

'Tea. It will help to cleanse you before they begin their work.'

'I don't need to be cleansed,' I say, feeling surprised and angry. 'I'm not the serial killer in this tent.'

The Half Face's eyes flash to me in an instant, and I recognize the warning that they convey.

'Do not translate that,' he growls to Batzorig.

The interpreter forces a smile. 'It is also just tea. Let it warm you, Juliet.'

I grudgingly take a sip and nearly spit it all out. The taste is beyond bitter. After I've forced myself to swallow it down, I can't suppress a shudder.

Tsend laughs. 'You do not like it,' Batzorig translates her words. 'Nobody does, at first. But it will give you a good, strong heart.'

*Well, I do need that,* I think.

Oyun rises from her fur and places herself behind the Half Face. She closes her eyes and extends her arms, her hands hovering close to his shaven head. She makes slow movements up and down, as if she is touching something invisible close to his skin. After a while, she begins a low, toneless humming.

I try to ignore the strange ritual at first. After all, I feel no sympathy for the Half Face's problems, and he doesn't deserve my attention. But then curiosity takes over and I openly stare at the gnarled, little woman, moving around this murderer so fearlessly. *Does she even know?* I wonder. Did anyone warn her and her daughter about the people they were going to receive? Maybe Batzorig told them one or two things of the whole truth, but I have a feeling that he doesn't want to risk my safety by spilling too much of the Half Face's secret.

Suddenly, Oyun stops. The chanting dies down and she lowers her arms, taking her place on the furs as if all she had done was pour herself another cup of tea. Everyone looks at her expectantly, except for Tsend, who seems to know what is going to happen and sits back with a relaxed smile on her face. The Half Face clenches his fists. I shrink back automatically; those fists have hurt me in more places than one, and I don't want to be anywhere near him if he decides to throw around another round of punches.

Oyun stares at him with her sunken, sky-bright eyes, clearly undisturbed by the newly formed tension in the round tent. She begins to speak; Batzorig clears his throat, nods a few times and then turns to the Half Face to translate her words.

'Oyun says that she felt a big disturbance in your spirit, but it is hard to tell where it is coming from exactly. She says...you may get ill when the real ceremony is over, or maybe during the ritual, if the spirit is vindictive. She also says...' He listened for a moment. 'She says it is going to hurt you. To prepare yourself, you must make peace with your body first.'

'What's that?' the Half Face says. He sounds hoarse.

'She tells me that there is a sweat lodge where you must sit. Your body must sweat to prepare for the ritual. Your mind must be undisturbed. This is essential.'

The Half Face nods. Oyun rises again and beckons for him to follow. For a moment, I wonder if I am supposed to say anything, but I can't think of a single sensible thing, so I just remain where I am, on the rugs on the floor, and watch him go.

Tsend points at me and asks me a question. I look to Batzorig for help.

'She says you look anxious. She would like to help you relieve some pain…'

'I'm not in pain,' I say, a little too quickly.

'That is what she calls it. Pain in your heart.'

'Oh.' If I'm honest, I don't really want to address that particular pain right now; it's like touching a bruise that is still too fresh.

'She wants to help you to relax. But it seems I will have to go.' Batzorig smiles and gets up. 'Enkhbad and I will have to return to the van anyway.'

'Go? But…what about us? What about me?'

'Don't worry, Juliet. We're going to retrieve the tents for the night, so you can stay here and relax. You'll be safe with Tsend.'

'I can't talk to her.'

'Maybe you can.' He smiles once more, and again I see the sadness in his eyes.

I turn my own eyes away. It's nice to have someone watching over me, I think, but right now he just makes me feel like a lost puppy. I'm not quite *that* helpless. I cannot be, because if I allow myself to remain scared and intimidated and alone, it will destroy me before this journey has come to an end.

# Chapter 10

## If I burn

Batzorig and Enkhbad exit the *ger* together, leaving me alone with Oyun's daughter. She holds up the kettle, offering me more of the same bitter tea. I shake my head, feeling mildly embarrassed. Tsend doesn't look too fazed. She downs her own cup in one gulp and seems to actually relish the sensation of her mouth shriveling up from the inside. When she rubs her belly theatrically and gives me a satisfied grin, I actually smile.

She crouches near me and says something, motioning for me to turn around. I'm not sure what she wants to do, but I obediently turn my back to her, so that I'm facing the tiny bench that Batzorig called a shrine.

Tsend brushes the strands of hair away from my neck and runs her fingers over the upper part of my spine, gently probing my skin and the first few vertebrae. Her hands are very warm and very strong, I notice. She sighs when she comes across a hard, painful knot in the muscles of my left shoulder, and I let out an involuntary groan. She makes a soothing noise, and then motions for me to take off my vest and long-sleeved T-shirt.

I hesitate. What if the Half Face swaggers back in? He would only have to take one look at me in my bra, and be all over me again. And what if he noticed the tiny chip that I'm still hiding inside my underwear?

Tsend sees me looking at the door of the *ger*, and seems to understand at least part of my worries. She closes the fabric tightly and makes a horizontal gesture with her arm. Even without knowing Mongolian, that's a clear sign: no one will come in.

'Alright,' I say, giving in. I free my arms from the vest and the T-shirt.

Tsend brushes down the straps of my bra, then unhooks it, letting her fingers travel over my back once again, discovering the tension just between my shoulders.

'Pain,' she says, surprising me so much that I almost jump. However, this seems to be about the only word of English that she knows, because she doesn't say anything else; she just pressed down on the muscles and repeats: 'Pain?'

I shrug. My back and my neck feel sensitive, but they're not exactly hurting. I just haven't been able to fully relax since the day of the hearing.

The shaman's daughter moves her hands over my body, rubbing and pressing my muscles, until I feel my blood rushing with new vigor, and I get all glowy and warm.

*I actually feel better*, I think.

When she's done, she fastens my bra again.

'Thank you,' I say, not sure if she can understand me.

Tsend smiles and nods. 'Man,' she says. She says something else, but it's either in Mongolian, or coated with such a heavy accent that I can't make out any of the words.

'I'm sorry. I don't know what you're saying.'

She points at me, then covers half her face with her hand, and puts the other hand to her heart.

*Do I love him?* I stare at her in horror, then start shaking my head vigorously.

She speaks again. This time her voice is full of soft sympathy. She reaches out and gently touches the yellowish bruises on my upper arm. All I can do is stare at them, too, and wince slightly when she brushes them with her fingertips. Her fingers move up to my hair, brushing through the strands. She takes a comb and starts to untangle the knots that have been there since the hotel in Ulaanbaatar. When my hair is all smoothed out, she braids the tresses into an intricate plait on my head.

Finally, she begins to hum. She has a warm, steady voice, weaving the foreign melody around me like a warm blanket. I'm sad that I have no way of talking to her without the interpreter, but settle for listening to her singing.

The peaceful air is broken when the tent flap moves aside and Oyun enters. To my relief, I see that she is alone, but her sudden entering is a sharp reminder that the Half Face is out here, somewhere close, and I quickly pull on my T-shirt and vest.


The Half Face only returns to the *ger* when the sun has sunk behind the mountains, leaving the steppe so dark that it seems like we've drowned. I do my best to ignore his presence. He seems content with sitting quietly, his legs crossed on a fur, staring into the fire of the stove with a faraway look.

I catch myself wondering how he spent his time in that sweat lodge. Did he think about his brother and sister, the ones he never returned to? Did he contemplate the many people he's hurt or killed in the past?

After a while, Enkhbad returns with Batzorig. They have brought along two roomy tents, and Oyun slowly moves from the stove to our furs to hand out bowls of some dinner that I cannot identify, carrying the food with her right hand, her left hand touching her elbow.

'This is the traditional way to serve food,' Batzorig explains to me, when he notices me watching the woman with curiosity. 'It is considered polite.'

'What is it?' I ask, meaning the food in my bowl. They look like light brown, rather shapeless dumplings.

'*Buuz.* It is filled with mutton. Go on, try it.'

I take a bite, tasting the meat, mixed with onions and garlic. It's actually not as bad as I had feared.

Oyun explains to us that she and Tsend will perform the real ritual tomorrow, at sunrise.

So we will have to sleep in the tents, I realize. A new knot is forming in my belly, tighter than the ones that Tsend massaged out. I wish Enkhbad had brought the van up to the *ger*; I would have been a lot more comfortable inside the metal walls and on the leather seats, but that is not my main concern. It is the Half Face that worries me. He hasn't tried anything quite so rash as to kiss me again, not since yesterday evening, when I locked myself in the bathroom in Ulaanbaatar. But I fear that this is only thanks to the presence of unsuspecting Enkhbad and my new, loyal protector Batzorig. He hasn't had the chance to spend time alone with me. I doubt he will allow me to sleep in the *ger*, with the other two women.

When Tsend offers me a drink, I expect more of the same, bitter tea. The liquid in the cup is milky white, however. I take a sip. Where the tea was almost too bitter to swallow down, this new drink is so sour that I can't help but pull a face. Batzorig grins, but Tsend looks a little disappointed. Seeing her expression, I quickly force the stuff down my throat.

'*Airag*,' Tsend says. She holds up the bottle.

'Fermented horse milk,' Batzorig explains to me, taking a gracious sip from his own cup. 'You're tasting the heart of Mongolia now, Juliet. Horses are everything to us; even their milk sustains us.'

I take another sip. Now that I know what to expect, the sour taste doesn't seem so bad anymore, and I'm able to swallow it with a smile. But the Half Face surprises me; he empties his cup in one go, licking his lips, obviously enjoying the beverage in the same way that I would down a cup of hot coco.

Enkhbad and Batzorig take it upon themselves to set up the tents near the *ger*. They will sleep in the one closest to the white, round home of Oyun and Tsend; the Half Face has claimed the far right tent for himself and for me. I only tried to ask him if I could sleep in the *ger* once. The look on his face made it painfully clear that he had no patience for my complaining.

We sit by the stove until the fire dies down, leaving nothing but a few glowing embers. Tsend and Oyun will have to wrap themselves in their furs if they want to stay warm tonight. I worry about our tent, and the cold night air.

Only after Enkhbad leaves for his makeshift bed, and Batzorig follows him shortly after, with one last worried look at me, the Half Face stands up and offers me his hand.

It's such an unexpectedly civil gesture that I stare at him in the dancing shadows. He's like a living shadow himself, only barely distinguishable from the real night.

I must have been too slow for his liking, for he grabs my hand roughly and yanks me up, almost causing me to trip over my own feet. I want to pull myself away from him at once, but he holds on tightly.

'Careful, Julie,' he says, his voice so quiet that I must be the only one able to hear it. 'You don't want to get lost on the steppe on your own.'

The only light comes from inside the *ger*, and from the flashlight that Batzorig or Enkhbad has turned on inside their own tent. I can just imagine how easy it is to wander off into the wrong direction, the hill rapidly blocking out even those two little specks of light, so that you can never retrace your steps back to the safety of the tents.

He guides me in the direction of our tent, suddenly halting in his tracks. I hear him mutter something, searching his pockets for something. A moment later, a small patch of darkness lights up with the artificial light of my phone.

I hadn't even thought of that. He directs the light at my face, making my skin glow ghostly pale. 'How about another picture?'

'Is that necessary?'

'Oh, Julie, think of where you *are*,' he chuckles. 'When this is all over, you can put them up on your Facebook wall.'

'It's way too dark, anyway.'

'I'll turn on the flash. Look.'

There's a flash and the sound of my phone snapping a photo.

I look. The picture is grainy and dark, but it's still me. 'Please don't do anything to me tonight.'

He looks at me without replying.

'I know what you want from me, but I can't...I don't want it.'

'It's cold here, Julie.' He takes my hand again and I stumble after him, with only the light from my phone to guide us to the far right, square tent. He zips it open and pushes me through the narrow opening, inside. He's not ungentle, but I feel my heart rate increase with every passing second.

There's a distinct smell of animal inside the tent, and not a lot of room to move. I fumble around for a flashlight and, once my hand hits the hard plastic object, hurry to turn it on.

There are two separate sleeping bags on the ground, and a new, unopened plastic water bottle in the corner. There's a canvas bag with my old clothes folded up inside of it. I'm grateful that Batzorig or Enkhbad remembered to take them out of the van for me. Not that I will be wearing a thin summer blouse or a skirt any time soon, not now that the Mongolian steppe turns out to be so cold and windy. But there is a strange comfort in seeing my own items, to be able to touch the fabric and think of my own wardrobe, my bedroom, and my home.

The Half Face closes the flap of the tent, at once expelling the cold air that was leaking in. The fabric of the tent isn't made of the flimsy material that I know from my few brief camping trips; it's almost as thick and sturdy as the fabric of the *ger*.

There's an awkwardly intimate atmosphere in this confined place. The yellow light of the flashlight only adds to that.

The Half Face doesn't look at me when he pulls off his boots, pulls down the zipper of his sleeping bag and wraps himself in it. I turn off the flashlight. Everything is engulfed in darkness, so intense that I can't tell the difference when I momentarily close my eyes.

I kneel down, removing my shoes by feeling where the laces are, then, feeling a bit embarrassed, I pull off my sweater and pants. I would sleep fully dressed, just as I did last night, but the clothes are so thick and impractical that I feel they'd strangle me in my sleep. And anyway, the Half Face can't see a thing now. All I have to do is get dressed before he wakes up tomorrow, or wait until he has left the tent.

As if he can sense my thoughts, his voice, filled with humor, pierces the dark tent. 'Are you naked now?'

'No!' I say, quickly rolling myself in my sleeping bag. 'Of course not.'

'Then what are you wearing? I could hear you take *some*thing off.'

'Just stop.'

'Can't you turn on the light-*ah*?'

'No.'

'Unbraid your hair?'

'No! Just go to sleep!'

'*Just* your hair, Julie,' he says smoothly. 'I won't even see you.' I hear the rustling of his sleeping bag as he sits back up, and before I can reply, his fingers tangle in my hair at the base of my skull. 'Or I'll do it. Let's call it a com-pro-*mise*,' he whispers, running his breath down my neck. 'Sit up.'

I do what he tells me. The skin of my head begins to tingle in a pleasant sort of way. I suppress a shiver; having my hair played with is usually such a good feeling. Chris used to do it all the time; he used to love running his hands through my hair slowly, brushing his fingertips against my scalp.

'You see? It's nice,' the Half Face mutters. He finds the end of the braid and starts to loosen the tresses one by one, spreading the hair over my shoulders as carefully as if he were arranging a bouquet of flowers.

When that is done, he lowers his hands from my head to my arms and lower back, exploring the edges of the long-sleeved T-shirt that I am still wearing, moving up again to trace his fingertips between my shoulders, to the exact spot where Tsend's hands found the painful knot in my muscles. Then he slides them up over my ribcage until they come to rest on the underwires of my bra, just below the swell of my breasts.

I swallow and close my eyes, even though it doesn't make a difference.

'Are you really going to scream if I do it?' he whispers. I can just hear the grin in his voice, mixed with something much darker.

'I will,' I whisper. 'I will scream.'

'No. You won't.'

His hand cups my left breast, covering it almost entirely. A sharp, quick pinch of electricity shoots through my body.

'Ooh, I feel you shudder.' He brings his mouth close to my ear. 'Isn't this much easier in the darkness, Juliet? Isn't it... almost like a secret thought-*ah*?'

'How can I make this clear to you?' I say, full of exasperation. 'I don't *want* you, I don't *like* you. My life is better without you in it.'

'Maybe for now, but that won't be true much longer. You'll see, Julie. You'll see shortly.' He removes his hand from my breast, and for a short moment I am able to breathe freely. Then he pushes me down on my side, my back still turned to him, leaving his arm to rest heavily on the upper side of my body, so I can't escape. His hand is in my neck, below my ear, where he tickles and brushes the delicate skin. 'Do you like the shaman, Julie? I may be free after tomorrow. How will you like me then, Jools? The new, unchained me? No more Black.'

I shake my head.

'No? What was that?'

'Black,' I mutter. 'That's not how it works. That's not how madness can be excused.'

'Ex*c*used, Juliet?'

I gulp and take a large breath of air. 'I think you're looking for a way to excuse and redeem yourself at the same time,' I say, though my voice is shaking. 'But you can't have both.'

Before I can take another breath, he rolls me on my

back and moves to sit on top of me, straddling my waist. His weight makes it difficult to breathe. I pull at his forearms, while the edges of my vision start to blur.

'There's – no – *Black!*' I gasp, in one final attempt to be brave. 'All of this – it's just *you.*'

His face sinks down so close that his lips almost brush mine; I feel it by the heat of his breath. I stop moving. The world starts spinning  when I finally feel his body weight shift.

I gulp and wheeze, my lungs struggling for a supply of fresh air.

'Black is real,' he whispers intensely. 'And he burns in my mind like a fire. But here's the thing, Juliet: from now on, if I burn – so will *you.*'

# Chapter 11

## The Black

Dawn breaks early the next morning. When I wake, the Half Face has already left his sleeping bag and is standing on the hilltop outside, looking over the steppe with an unreadable expression on his black-and-white face.

I use this moment to dress hastily. The air chills my body before I slip into my warm sweater. I run my hands through the loose tresses of my hair, brushing them as well as I possibly can. Maybe I can ask Tsend to lend me a comb later.

They are waiting for us behind the *ger*. Tsend is wearing a wide, blue tunic that covers her feet, adorned with yellow and red ribbons. Her neck and arms are wrapped with beaded strings, her head is crowned with feathers. Oyun is hardly recognizable behind a mask from which two cow's horns protrude into the air. When she turns around, I notice two staring eyes embroidered on the mask. It is slightly disconcerting to behold.

Both Oyun and Tsend are holding a large, round drum in their arms.

Batzorig greets us with a weak smile. I don't see Enkhbad anywhere, but maybe he is still sleeping in his tent. I wish I could go back and catch another hour of undisturbed rest myself, but at that moment, the Half Face slips his arm around my waist, pulling me close to him as we make the short descent from the hill to the low valley behind the *ger*, where the two shamans and our interpreter are waiting for us.

'You must sit over there,' Batzorig tells the Half Face. 'Juliet, you can sit here with me.'

'What do I have to do?' the Half Face asks, as he sits down where the interpreter directed him. His fists rest in his lap; he is nervous, I realize.

'Do nothing now. If something changes, I will tell you.'

He nods. 'How long will it take?'

Batzorig shrugs. 'As long as it takes. They can't tell me – it may be an hour. May be a day.'

I shiver at the thought of having to be out here in the cold for an entire day, but I sit down on the ground all the same, my legs curled up beneath me.

The two shamans position themselves behind my captor. Tsend raises her drum and begins to beat a low, steady rhythm: *thump. Thump-thump. Thump.* Like the heartbeat of a sleeping person.

Batzorig takes his place next to me. He looks like he wants to say something, but then Oyun raises her voice to an eerie pitch, lifting her masked head to the cloud-hung sky. She is like a wounded creature shrieking out in pain, and I can't help but shift back, the hairs on my arms and my neck standing up. Tsend begins to mutter something, her hands never resting as she beats her drum. The Half Face is starting to look scared.

Suddenly, Oyun grabs both sides of his head in her claw-like hands and says something in her normal voice, repeating it again and again.

'What's she saying?' I whisper to Batzorig.

'She's searching for the presence of the spirit,' he mutters back. 'She says: state your name.'

The Half Face stares at Oyun's face, so close to his own, but he can't or won't reply. Nothing else happens. Finally, the shaman seems to decide on a different strategy, because she pulls back her hands and starts muttering along with her daughter. Gradually, the muttering turns to singing.

I watch this strange scene with a mixture of fear and genuine awe. After a couple of minutes, Oyun breaks off her singing abruptly and asks a sharp question. Batzorig immediately translates: 'She wants to know if you have any close ancestors that may burden you.'

'My mother was a dear and my father was a brute,' the Half Face replies through clenched teeth.

'Are they alive or dead?'

'*Dead-ah.*'

It occurs to me with a shock that he might have come back, when his face had been filled with ink and his heart with revenge. I'm not even sure that I feel sorry for his dad.

'Oyun says...there may be something connected to your anger. Something that has to do with your family.'

'Why do you think I'm *here?*'

Batzorig says something in Mongolian. It is Tsend who answers with a short shake of her head.

'They think you need to contemplate on your anger before they can call out a spirit.'

'His name is Black,' the Half Face growls. 'I *know* him. Now. Get. Him. Out!'

'Fine. This will hurt.'

'Then make it *hurt*.'

I'm shocked to see Oyun pulling out a whip from somewhere. It's not an ordinary riding crop, the ones I'd expect from a people who spend most of their lives on horseback, but a mean device with several long, leather strokes.

'You must stand up now,' Batzorig says. 'And don't move. It's also important that you remain absolutely quiet. Not even a whisper of pain. Do you understand this?'

The Half Face's eyes lock on the whip in Oyun's hand, but he nods briefly. I feel myself getting nauseous. Are they honestly going to beat him now?

'Take off your coat and shirt,' Batzorig says, after listening to Oyun.

He does it without speaking. Despite our close proximity in the last few days, this is the first time that I actually see him undress. The tattoos don't stop on his neck; they swivel down his toned torso like coiling snakes; black, white, yin, yang, as though even his own body is constantly struggling for a balance between good and evil.

Without warning, Oyun lashes out at him. The whip hits his body with a soft thwack at first, but then rapidly increases in speed, until I clearly hear the sound of the leather connecting with his flesh. I look on with my heart in my throat. The drum rumbles and roars as the whip comes down again and again.

I close my eyes, but snap them back open when the sound suddenly stops.

'Juliet,' Batzorig says. 'It's your turn.'

'My...turn?' I repeat, stunned. Have they all lost their minds? I jump up, ready to flee to the *ger*. I'm suddenly more scared than I was last night, with the Half Face's hands caressing my body. 'No – tell them no! I am not going to be whipped!'

'She means that you have to *do* it,' Batzorig says quickly, a look of mortification flashing across his face. 'I'm sorry, I misinterpreted.'

'Oh.' I sink down again, feeling the rush of my panicked heartbeat decrease. 'Why?'

'Because your energy is...conflicting. It burdens him. It is *you* that needs to purify him.'

'Why in God's name would I do that?' I ask, making my voice intentionally loud, so that the Half Face can clearly hear the contempt in it. 'You know what he did! You know what I am, Batzorig; I'm his hostage. And so are you! And Enkhbad, and Oyun and Tsend, and they don't even *know* it!'

Tsend stops her drumming and walks over to me. She looks at me with that same pity that I detected in her last night. She doesn't know who I am, or what is going on, but she did see my bruises. She might be able to take a guess in the right direction. Not that it will help me, or her, if I do anything that angers the Half Face. The shaman's daughter speaks to me softly, gesturing to the whip with her hands.

After a while, Batzorig says: 'He needs you to punish him for his wrongdoings. Only that will clear the darkness.'

'Well, I can't do it,' I say, the fear spilling over me again, clenching an invisible hand around my throat. 'He will never forgive me and he'll find some horrible way to punish me.'

'Perhaps he won't. He *needs* this.'

'He just thinks he does.'

'Isn't that enough?'

I look at the Half Face. His skin doesn't look much different from before; Oyun's arms do not have the strength to beat a man such as himself until he is raw and bleeding. There's nothing I can do to help myself, I think, and for all his good intentions, Batzorig is still just a prisoner himself. The chip in my bra is my only consolation, but it didn't help me last night. It won't help me the next time that the Half Face decides to punish *me* for something as insolent as doubting his sanity.

But at least I can give him a good beating for it.

Without saying another word, I get up and take the whip in my hands. I walk over to where he is standing, for once meeting his gaze without flinching.

'Are you going to scream if I do it?' I ask, repeating the words he said to me last night.

A taut grin spreads from one half of his face to the other. 'Any attention from *you* is good attention, Juliet.'

'I hate you!' I spit at him. 'I don't hate Black, and I don't hate your father, and I don't hate the men that did this to you, but I just simply *hate you!*'

'Go ahead, Julie,' he whispers. 'Do whatever you have to do. But when you drag yourself back from that edge, don't tell me that I did not give you what you *need-ah.*'

I swing my arm back and hit him square in the chest. Despite the shaman's warning to remain as still as possible, the Half Face hisses in pain. This sound awakens a deep, satisfyingly dark urge in me to hit harder. And I do; I put all my strength into the next blow - all the power that Oyun couldn't muster. Well, I am still young, and I am strong, and this man is going to suffer for every bit of misery that he has thrown my way.

I hardly notice that Tsend has picked up her drum again, and that she is beating it in the same rhythm I use to lash out at the Half Face. Oyun sends her chilling songs to the sky. If there really is something like the Black, I'm sure that he cannot deny us any longer; but if there isn't, this is just a morbid display of human madness.

I don't care either way. I'm getting what I need. In that, the Half Face was right.

The drumming stops as abruptly as it began, and I find myself faltering in my movements, my arm somewhere halfway between me and my captor. I'm panting, sweating. But that is still nothing compared to the mess that the Half Face is in. His breath comes out in ragged wheezes, his chest is bleeding; no longer black and white, but red and swollen. His eyes are closed and his jaws clench tightly. Even his fists are shaking.

Tsend beckons me. Obediently, I step back, a little dizzy from the trance I had gotten myself into. Oyun approaches the Half Face with a jug. Before I can ask what is going to happen now, she splashes the beaten man with water. His body jerks, as if he has just received an electrical shock.

'*Nergüi! Nergüi!*' Oyun cries. Tsend joins in, shrieking close to his ear. '*Nergüi!*'

'What are they doing now?' I whisper to Batzorig.

'They're giving him a new name,' he mutters back. 'Nergüi – it means No Name. When a man has no name,' he explains, seeing my puzzled expression, 'a spirit cannot latch on to him as easily. It's a diversion.'

When the two women finally seem satisfied, Oyun takes off her mask and sits on the ground. Her eyes are closed. Tsend rolls her shoulders and nods to us, smiling, then begins to talk.

'She says it is done.' Batzorig rakes his hand through his hair. 'She says the both of you may feel tired or drained for a while. The energy has been stirred; you need time for it to settle into its new pattern. Like disturbed water in a lake.'

'I think what he needs more is a first aid kit,' I mutter. 'No, you don't have to translate that.'

'There's a first aid kit back in the van.'

But he will have to walk back a couple of painful kilometers before he can even reach the van, I think. I watch as the Half Face crouches down on a jutting rock, his head resting on his arms. He's still panting. I'm not entirely sure why I do it, but after a moment I get up and walk over to him.

'Juliet.' He must have heard my footsteps. 'Did that *satisfy* you?'

'Yes.' I'm not going to lie. After a second, I carefully sit down next to him; not close enough that he can touch me, but still near enough that our conversation will remain private. 'Will you hurt me for this?'

He shakes his head.

'Is it…is it gone now?'

Finally, he moves his head to look at me. He seems beyond exhausted, as if he has been forced to run up a mountain, instead of having to stand still while the lashes of the whip rained down on him. I feel a little sick to my stomach, now that the worst fury is over.

'I don't know if he's gone,' the Half Face rasps. He lets out a barking laugh that stops just as suddenly. 'I'm too sore to tell. What do *you* think, Julie?'

'You're going to hurt me if I say it.'

'Nooo. No, Julie. Not this time.'

'Do you swear?'

'Swear?' He looks at me as if I've just asked him to fly to the moon. For a while, I don't know if he's going to laugh or shout at me, but then he surprises me by shrugging. 'Alright, Julie, I won't hurt you. Cross my heart and hope to *die*.'

'Okay. Well. I told you before. I don't really believe in spirits. I...I don't believe in Black. I think you're somehow...damaged... Or maybe you were born this way, like a psychopath. Beating you and chanting and drumming, none of that is going to cure you. You need a real doctor, because you're not possessed. You are just wired this way, to be...'

'A *freak?*' he interrupts me with a dangerous growl. He leans over me, gripping my face with both his hands and forcing me to look at him. 'So I'm doomed to be a freak, am I, Jools?'

My heart is immediately hammering away in panic. 'You said you wouldn't hurt me!'

'This isn't hurting you.' His fingers still press into my face. His thumb moves over my cheekbone. 'No – listen, look. I'm not born to be a monster. Where would *that* leave the world, Juliet? Tell me that.'

'I'm not saying that you're –'

'Yes. You *are*. It's alright.' He releases me, but doesn't move away much. 'You've been born blessed, haven't you? Clever. Pretty. Pri-vi-leged.' He smiles. 'I bet your mommy and your daddy still love each other very much.'

'No, they don't,' I say. I don't know why I feel inclined to tell him something so personal. 'My dad left my mom to care for me and my sister on her own after they'd been shouting at each other for three years. You're not the only one with a sob story.'

To my surprise, he lets out another rasping laugh that quickly dies down. 'Nobody has cried over my story, Juliet. But maybe *you* will. What do you think? You can be my Crying Madonna.'

'I'm too angry for that.'

'Maybe one day you will be sad for me.'

I look at him, long and hard. 'And be your messiah?'

'You could be. Chase the crazy out of my head.'

I shake my head, but his words stick with me, like they're a tiny, ringing bell. I have no means to defend myself against him if it comes down to physical strength. There's not much use for screaming either; whatever I do to resist him, he will just take out on me  by cutting the air from my throat again. Besides, he still has that gun. He might shoot Tsend and Oyun in their *ger*, or he could fire a bullet at Enkhbad or Batzorig. Even if he doesn't aim to kill, the absence of a hospital and the exposure to the elements on this lonely steppe will certainly take care of that. I don't think he will shoot at *me*. But I can't bear the thought of someone else getting punished, just because I can't take a deep breath and allow his hands to explore my body.

This is a death-trap he's got me in, I realize. He has maneuvered me in exactly the right position: too weak to fight him, too far away from home to escape, and too dependent on the friendliness of others to willingly put them in danger.

But I know now that I do have a different kind of weapon that I can employ. I possess something that the Half Face craves, something he needs as badly as I need air, and he can't force it out of me. The real thing that he needs from me is his redemption.

# Chapter 12

## Sorry isn't good enough

'Talk to Gansükh,' Tsend tells us the next morning, after we have risen with the sun. I have hardly been able to sleep, the images of the day still dancing through my head like tiny devils. My only relief had been that the Half Face was too sore and too exhausted to repeat his actions of the night before. Even though his arm went up around my waist, and he held me close to him like I was his one true love, he never touched me in places that he shouldn't try to touch me. He hadn't even spoken at first – not to me, anyway. I had heard him mumbling snippets of sentences and half-finished words for hours. His voice had risen and fallen in such an agitated way that it had begun to scare me, and I had moved to try and cover my ears.

Once he had felt me stirring, he'd sounded a lot more composed. The sudden change was baffling.

'I woke you.'

'I was still awake,' I had said. 'But you're scaring me. Please, let me go. I can sleep in the *ger* with Oyun and Tsend.'

His arm had only held me tighter. 'If I don't hold on to something, I will fall.'

'Do you really think that there's a way *down* from where you are?'I ask.

'Yes there is, Juliet,' he had said quietly. 'There's a long, fast drop.'

I had said nothing in reply to that, and he had fallen silent. His steady breathing rose and fell behind me. I could feel it very well, my back closely pressed to his chest, his nose near my neck. It had taken me hours to fall asleep, but eventually I'd slipped into unquiet dreams. What worried me most, the next morning, was how much I had loved the warmth of his body close to mine in those brief minutes before I was fully awake and the cold air of predawn seeped into our tent.

Now we're standing on the hillside, gathered before the *ger*. They have given us *airag* and *buuz* to sustain us along the way. I'm still shivering, even though the sun has managed to climb above the horizon entirely, and I'm once again wrapped up in my warm and insulating traveling clothes.

'Gansükh is the strongest shaman in all the land,' Tsend says, translated by Batzorig. 'He will not like to talk,' she adds. 'He is a lonely man, he does not like to receive people; especially not tourists. But he is *real*. He will be able to help you.'

'Why didn't they get the spirit out of him?' I ask Batzorig.

The interpreter looks uncomfortable. 'Oyun says that he is too strong. The injustice runs deeper than she had anticipated.'

'The injustice?' I mutter. 'I don't understand. Black is supposed to be an entity. Isn't he?' I ask the Half Face.

He nods, but he doesn't look as convinced as before.

'It is complicated,' Batzorig says. 'Oyun tells me that sometimes, a spirit is like a person without a body. And sometimes it is an ancestor. And some other times, it is like the energy of a past event, surrounding us and shaping us – defining us in a very real way. This can be good, and then there is no need to relieve ourselves of it. Or it can be dark, and we seek to free ourselves from what it is that hurt us so much. Gansükh can help him, she says.'

He pauses and asks a question in Mongolian. When Oyun replies, his face suddenly falls. He looks older and grayer, the lines in his weathered face more pronounced than before.

'What?' I say, my heart at once hammering a worried beat. 'Did she say something bad?'

'I asked where Gansükh lives. She said he belongs to the Reindeer People.'

'Who are where?'

'Far away,' he says. 'Far across the steppe, up in the mountains. If they are there at all. They are nomads; they travel.'

I turn to the Half Face with a sinking feeling in my stomach, as though I'm dropping off the edge of a cliff. 'You can't do this. It's too much.'

He looks back at me with doubt written over his starkly contrasting face. Could it be that he is actually listening to me? Maybe I can talk him out of this.

'Even for you, this is an insane journey,' I go on, my voice pleading. 'We don't even know where this man is, or how long it will take to reach the mountains. Let's...let's just turn around now and go home. I'm so tired – aren't you?'

'I came here for one purpose only.' He pauses, looking over the hill and across the steppe, not really fixing his eyes on anything in particular. He's quiet for a long while, and again I allow myself to be carefully optimistic. My hope is crushed when he shakes his head. 'I can't leave before that is done.'

He might as well have taken a hammer and smashed my heart. I am so broken that I hardly notice the look on Batzorig's face, or the worried whispers of Oyun and Tsend.

'Please,' I hear myself say, but distantly, as if I'm a spectator, looking at a scene performed by strangers. I already know that the begging is hopeless. 'God, please, just take me home. I can't do this anymore; I don't want to go on!'

That is when the Half Face does something unexpected. He turns to me and wraps his arms around my body, almost entirely enveloping me. He doesn't hold on tight, just tenderly, almost like a father with his newborn child. 'I'm sorry,' he whispers. 'I am so, so sorry.'

I don't try to fight him off. I am frozen in my place, stiff from homesickness and longing and frustration and trepidation.

'Juliet,' he says again, in a voice that is even rawer than usual, and barely audible. 'I really *am* sorry.'

That's when I manage a small shake of the head, and somehow find the place where my body has locked up my voice. 'Sorry isn't good enough.'

Tsend embraces me long and hard before we say goodbye. She takes my head in her two hands and looks at me, surveying my face, my eyes. I wonder if she can see how sick I'm feeling on the inside. She smiles, though it doesn't seem to reach her eyes, and she says something that sounds like a reassurance. I just shake my head.

When we walk back to the van, I feel like I'm ready to cry. I don't. I keep it in, forcing my burning eyes to remain dry. It's hard; I have to keep my jaws clenched together so tightly that they start hurting, and I have to keep my eyes fixed on the road ahead without so much as glancing at the Half Face.

Enkhbad has grown silent along the way. Batzorig has spoken to him in short, fast sentences, and since then, his playful smile has been wiped right off his face. We reach the van in silence, but when the Half Face opens the door and gestures for me to get in, the driver suddenly shakes his head, turns around and points an accusing finger at my captor.

'What?' the Half Face snaps. His mood has dropped to dangerous lows ever since I didn't accept his apology.

Batzorig licks his lips nervously. He doesn't translate Enkhbad's words, but sounds like he's trying to convince him, seeming almost as agitated as the Half Face was last night.

Enkhbad doesn't seem to like what he is hearing. He shakes his head again, and his voice rises even higher.

'If there's a problem, you TELL ME NOW!' the Half Face suddenly roars.

I jump. I haven't heard him shout since the negotiations with the police in Fallhallow.

There are tiny beads of sweat on Batzorig's face. 'Enkhbad is concerned about this trip,' he says, though I'm sure that "concerned" isn't how our driver has described his current emotions. 'It's too unexpected. He doesn't have a map, and he hasn't been paid to take you much further than Oyun.'

'And who's paying him, hm? How much money do you two get? *You* know, Batzy, but does *he* know? Aah – I don't. Think. So.'

'It's not just the money,' Batzorig says, growing more nervous by the second. 'He has other engagements, and so do –'

'No, *you* don't.' The Half Face lets out a rough laugh. 'And I would think again about that money; you're dismissing payment so ea-*si*-ly. See, Batman, the Mongolian Police Force or Fallhallow's best and brightest moustaches or the United Nations or whatever, they're all paying you to stick this one out and return Juliet safely home. *I'm* offering you so much more than just money. *I'm* offering to pay with your *lives-ah*.'

From where he pulled that gun so suddenly, I don't know. But it's there in his hand now, and he's waving it about like a flag, pointing it at me, at Batzorig and at Enkhbad in random order. The effect is immediate. Batzorig stops moving altogether; I feel a familiar, cold fear creep through my body, starting in my abdomen, paralyzing my feet. Enkhbad's face drains of all color, his eyes staring stupidly at the pitch-black firearm.

'Yeah, go ahead and translate that,' the Half Face chuckles. 'It's time we let him in on our little secret, isn't it – Juliet-*ah*?'

Hearing my name unlocks me from my frozen state, and I begin to shake my head, but the Half Face simply waves his gun again, and I stop. 'Go ahead, talk. TALK! EXPLAIN HOW MUCH OF A MONSTER I AM!'

Seeing no other option, our interpreter turns to Enkhbad and begins to explain. He talks slowly and quietly. I can see how he has to take a gulp of air between every sentence. How he is trying to relax his hands, while he really wants to clench them into two nervous fists. I recognize all these signs of suppressed fear, because I have found myself in that place over and over again in these past few days.

When he is done, Enkhbad stares at us as if he is seeing us for the first time. I can't imagine what we must look like to him; having transformed from an eccentric, young couple into a dangerous, insane criminal with underworld tattoos all over his body and one scared, helpless little girl. The worst is that Batzorig, who knew the truth all this time, didn't give him a single warning.

I want to say *I'm sorry*, like all of this is somehow my fault. Before I can open my mouth, the driver lets out an animalistic howl, one that scares my heart right out of my throat. He lurches forward, his arms outstretched to the Half Face.

He is a big, heavily built man, so I can see why he thinks that strangling him might stand a chance. Maybe he is filled with such a terrible, justified rage, that he has forgotten the gun that my captor is still holding. Or maybe he thinks that raw physical force can defeat a bullet, fired from up close, by the grace of God.

Either way, he is wrong.

Batzorig cries out a warning when Enkhbad crashes into the Half Face and a loud bang pierces the quiet of the steppe. I want to scream, but my throat is clenched tight, so I'm just standing on buckling knees, my mouth gaping wide, with no sound escaping my lips.

Enkhbad staggers back. He looks more confused than scared. My eyes sweep over his entire body; his shirt, his pants, his face – nowhere do I detect a trace of blood.

'*Missed* you!' the Half Face hisses. He takes one large step forward and shoves the driver down on the ground. The man is too shocked to put up a fight. He falls to the ground, just before the Half Face's feet, staring up at him.

The Half Face kicks him in the stomach.

'Stop!' Batzorig says. 'You won. We'll go – we're going to Gansükh.'

The Half Face doesn't listen to him. He raises the gun and points it steadily at Enkhbad's face, his finger tightening around the trigger.

I can't take it. I just *can't.* This is too much like Fallhallow National Bank, and I feel like I'm back on the floor, unable to move but also unable to shut my eyes to block out the slaughter. Only this time, I already know what kind of monster is swinging that gun around, what the sound will be like when he fires another shot, and what a dead body looks like from up close.

And I can't let that happen another time.

I find a little strength in my legs and use it to cross the distance between me and the fallen driver as quickly as I can. The Half Face's arm is partially outstretched and I grab it with both my hands, pulling it away from Enkhbad, and maneuvering myself between him and the weapon before the Half Face can shoot.

'No,' I say, panting hard. I pull the hand with the gun to my own heart and stare at the Half Face's bright, shocked eyes. 'If you want to shoot someone – go ahead, shoot me. But you won't, will you?'

He doesn't reply. He seems too shocked at my sudden action to do anything at all.

I close my eyes. 'You won't. Because you need me. And you need *him* to drive the van, and you need Batzorig to translate for us. So, what are you going to do? Listen to Black? Or listen to me?'

I look at him again. That last remark seems to strike a chord, because he looks down at my chest, where the gun is still resting between my breasts, and jerks his arm away. A nauseous look creeps over his face.

'Good,' I breathe. I can't even count my heartbeats, that's how much it is raging.

'So, that's it, huh?' the Half Face says. 'The buddy road trip? Everybody needs each other now?'

'Well, not *everybody.*'

'*No?*' His voice drops to a sudden growl, low and dangerous, like a wolf's warning. 'You think so, Julie? You think you can dispose of me? Hm?' He grabs my arm. I close my eyes at once, expecting  his hand to grab my wrist until it almost breaks. Instead, he forces the cold steel of the gun into my hand. My eyes snap open.

'Then do it.' He brings my hand – gun and all – to his head. Then he opens his mouth, puts the gun in, so that it is pointing at the back of his throat. This way, he can't speak anymore, but his eyes bore into mine so hard that it almost hurts.

*Go on,* those eyes tell me, challenging me. *Do it. Shoot me, Julie, right through the head. It will be the end of a-a-a-ll of your troubles.*

And just like when I took the whip in my hands, I am overtaken by a burning hot desire to give in to his words and watch as his body falls to the ground and his blood spills from his head. He would never torment me again. We would be free, right now. Completely free.

Except for this black hatred that seems to latch on to my heart with every passing second that I'm relishing the thought of murdering my captor. Perhaps this is what he calls Black, I think. Perhaps it's not so difficult to become the Half Face.

I struggle to take a step back and throw the gun on the ground, between our feet. It's too hard to tell how he feels right now; when I look up, there's a mix of relief and anger and something else in his eyes. He doesn't say anything.

'It's not because I want to be with you,' I say. 'But I don't want to become you, either. I'm not going to let you break me, one way or the other.'

When I climb into the backseat of the van, the unreadable stare has turned into a look of utter bewilderment on his face.

# Chapter 13

## Drifting

The little green van is adrift on the steppe, like a lost boat on the sea. Enkhbad has gone nearly mute, driving the vehicle with his hands clenched around the steering wheel. I can tell he is terribly afraid, even if he doesn't say so. He must have at least a vague idea of the route, because he keeps heading towards a dark, protruding mountain, which from this distance looks like a two-headed horse. I hope he knows how to get to the Reindeer Herders. And I hope we'll get there soon.

I eat cold *buuz*, Oyun and Tsend's gift to us, until that's gone and we have to rely on our driver's cooking skills. His supply of food is steadily decreasing.

During the long days, I stick to Batzorig for company. I do notice how the Half Face is throwing me looks every few hours; sometimes he even stares at me for minutes on end, but he never talks to me anymore. I gladly make use of it and ignore his presence as well as I possibly can.

For a week, all we do is drive as long as daylight permits us, then stop at a random place to wait out the hours of darkness. The land is invariably beautiful, no matter where we pitch our tents: a lake so undisturbed that it reflects the sky like a mirror; a hillside with a herd of wild horses, keeping their wary distance while they tolerate our presence; a vale in a thousand shades of green, where the sunset crashes the heavens into such intense colors that it's like the sky is bleeding; patches of wood filled with dark pine trees and slim, silvery birches that balance on the flowing landscape like ballerinas.

Every night, as I wrap myself up and listen to the wind whistling around the mountains, the Half Face comes to lie next to me, pulling my body close to his through the synthetic fabric of the sleeping bags. He doesn't speak, but sometimes he runs his fingers through my hair when he thinks I'm asleep, brushing it tenderly.

I'm always awake until I can tell from his steady breathing that he's fallen asleep.

Dawn comes early in the empty land, but one morning, I awake with a startled feeling before the sun has had a chance to break free from the horizon. For a few moments, I can't tell what has unsettled me so much, or what is causing the restless feeling in my belly. I listen to the sounds around me; the Half Face breathing close behind me, his breath tickling the back of my neck, and the constant low and high cries of the wind. Those sounds I have grown familiar with.

It's the heavy roar of the engine that I can't place; not this early in the morning, at least. I sit up. My movement awakens the Half Face, who lies there listening for just a single heartbeat before he rushes past me, ripping open the tent and pulling away the fabric like there's a fire in his sleeping bag. I untangle myself from my own sleeping bag and follow him out, my heart racing like the wild horses that we watched cantering past us the other day, because I already know what is happening before I see it.

As I crawl outside and straighten up to a standing position, Batzorig emerges from his tent, pale and with a shocked expression on his unshaven face.

All we can do is watch as the van speeds away from us. It's faster than any of us can run, even if we put all our strength into it. As sudden as the engine woke me, the van turns behind the next slope of the hill, and disappears from sight. The engine sounds die away just as fast, and within a few minutes we are once again left alone with the wind.

'He left us,' I whisper. For once, I forget my fear and my hatred for the Half Face as I look up at him, desperate to find some kind of reassurance. 'And he took...he took the car.'

Instead of answering me, the Half Face turns to our interpreter, anger distorting his already messed-up face. 'Did you just let him *slip* away?'

'I wasn't watching him like some kind of prisoner!' Batzorig retorts.

'Oh, you noticed the looks he was giving us the last few days!'

'You mean the look of utter terror? Yes, we have all seen that. Look around and take a good look at Juliet, why don't you? You'll see her looking just like that, and *she*'s not running off.'

The Half Face closes in on him, raising his hands slowly, as if he's ready to wrap them around Batzorig's neck to squeeze more insolent words he might be holding in directly out of him.

'Stop.' I want to shout, but I can only rasp.

To my own surprise, the Half Face does stop moving. He doesn't quite turn around, but his hands fall back to his side.

'Juliet, get back in the tent. Now-*ah.*'

'No,' I say. 'The car's gone. The food is gone. We're out here in the middle of nowhere – how's a *tent* going to save us?'

He turns to face me fully now. He crosses the distance between us, grabbing both my shoulders in such a firm grip that I automatically wince, even before the actual pain hits me.

'Are you accusing me?'

'That's...that's not my point! What I'm *saying* is – listen! I'm telling you, we're in trouble.' I stare back at him without looking away. 'It doesn't matter who's got the gun and who's the hostage, because...look around!' I spread my arms wide and let out a hoarse laugh. 'There's nobody here, no one cares! No police, no hotel staff, no family. Not even Oyun and Tsend. We're *alone* and we're in trouble.'

'Juliet's right.' Batzorig shrugs helplessly and casts a look around. I know he's not seeing anything more hope-inspiring than I am.

The Half Face licks his lips, studies my face for another

few moments, and I can't read his expression at all. Then he releases my shoulders, pushing me back as if everything is my fault.

I stagger, but stay on my feet.

'The tents will give us shelter, at least,' Batzorig says. 'I have some biscuits stored in mine. Do you?'

'Just a few crumbs,' I say, a feeling of desperation washing over me like a cold wave. 'And only half a bottle of water. We have to go back to Oyun and Tsend – if we walk real fast, then maybe...'

'No.'

We both turn to the Half Face, who's standing a couple of feet away from me with a hard look on his face.

'But we must,' I say.

'There. The mountain. We're going *there.*'

'You can't be that insane!' I'm suddenly shouting, shaking my clenched fists at him. 'We have no idea what is up there; there might be noth –'

'The shaman is up there, Juliet, so we are going.'

I breathe in deeply. 'There might be *nothing.* The Herders could be gone. Gansükh could be *dead.* It might be too damn far to walk, and it could very well be too damn cold to even try.'

'I'm not giving up because that slit-eye turned and

ran,' he barks.

'Then go!' I throw my arms in the air. 'Go, and see if I care! Don't ever come back, you'd do the world a favor. But let us do the only sensible thing and walk back while we still have a chance!'

The Half Face lets out a humorless laugh. 'Oh, I'm not letting you walk off, Juliet. I need you.'

'FOR WHAT?' I shout, my voice rising even higher. 'What do you think I am, Half Face? Your redemption? Your Crying Madonna? Am I just a pretty face that you stole for your own pleasure – what?! And what...' I have to pause my shouting to take in a gulp of fresh air, '...what use do I have for you – for *any* of that, when I AM DEAD!?'

He turns around and starts tearing the pegs out of the earth, making the tent sag like a crumbling house. He drags the sleeping bags outside, tossing the flashlight after it. Batzorig and I stand by, looking helplessly at his rage. It's too dark to move on now, even with the meager lights from the flashlights. I wrap my arms around myself and shiver. I haven't even gotten fully dressed myself, and the cold is piercing. Batzorig wraps his arm around my shoulders, giving me a little of his warmth. I lean into him, feeling the full impact of Enkhbad's escape hitting me with the weight of granite.

'It's not hopeless, Juliet,' Batzorig says. 'We may run into a couple of *gers* any day. We can find herders and hunters.'

'And then what?' I ask. 'He's not going to let us stay anywhere. We'll have to follow him to that mountain.'

'Listen.' He hesitates, opening his mouth wordlessly, as though he can't decide on the right words. 'It might be over sooner than you think. The Mongolian –'

He falls silent as soon as he spots the Half Face making his way back to us, with both our tent and the other one rolled up and wrapped under his arm. 'Get your hands off my girl. Carry this.'

He thrusts the tent at the interpreter, who is forced to let me go.

I wish Batzorig would finish his sentence, but I can't even ask him. The Half Face takes my arm in his, almost like he's supporting me to walk, even though I can stand on my own two feet just fine. He sets off, and we do the only thing we can do; we follow the man down the hill, on to the next.

# Chapter 14

## For I have sinned

The hunger quickly takes its toll on me. My head spins regularly, and makes the earth feel like the deck of a ship rocked by waves. Batzorig sometimes has to grab my arm to keep me from falling, and I bite the inside of my cheek, hoping that the pain will keep my mind clear.

When it's not my empty stomach that weighs me down, it is the constant feeling of trepidation; of walking around in circles or the sense of being headed for an unattainable horizon, one that constantly skips back as soon as we think we have gotten a little closer to the edge of the world.

The edge – that is where the mountains are. That's where the big, two-headed horse beckons us, and laughs at us, and remains silent.

I get sores under my feet that transform the act of walking from an unpleasant activity to torture, and I'm constantly out of breath. Only now do I realize how easy it was to cross this landscape sitting in a car, leaning back in the leather seats while the engine did all the hard work for us. I come to the conclusion that I have been shamefully out of shape for years. After climbing just one hill, my chest seems to be on fire.

So bleak are the days that I'm almost grateful for the nights. They are still much the same, with the exception of a warm dinner. Batzorig rations his biscuits for a while, but even they can't last longer than a couple of days, if we each take one bite every evening. He also found a couple of matches, somewhere tucked away in a hidden corner of his bag. We've been making small fires ever since; fires that get us through the evening, but not through the entire night. Most of the time, the wood we find is so moist that we sit in smoking fumes more than we get to warm our hands on actual flames. Still, it's a blessing every time we stop and make camp.

The tent becomes my only form of shelter, and I start

loving it for that. My sleeping bag is no longer confining, but is a warm cocoon, something to snuggle into, to hold me when I'm sinking into an exhausted sleep. Even the Half Face's arms around my waist are becoming better at comforting me than scaring me. They, too, are warm and strong – something to keep me from falling into complete depression or panic. One night, I even break from my usual position of facing the tent wall and keeping my back to my captor as he wraps me in his embrace, and roll onto my other side. My head rests under his chin, and I can feel his breath tickle down through my hair. His sudden jerk tells me that he is surprised, but I'm beyond caring. I am too cold, too sore, too scared to think about rules of propriety.

He smells of grass and smoke.

'How are you so sure we're going to make it?' I ask, not bothering to look up or open my eyes. The complete darkness wouldn't show me his face anyway, nor his shockingly bright blue eyes that always send a jolt through my belly, or the fact that he hasn't shaven for days and there's a stubble of dark hair growing on his jaws and on his head.

'I'm *not* sure.'

'Then why are you so determined?' I'm too tired to

even feel angry anymore. 'Don't you get scared?'

'I got plenty scared in my life, Jools. And the scariest thing I've ever known is right in here.'

'In where?'

His fingers slide from my waist to my wrist, and he directs my hand to his chest, where I can feel the steadily beating heart underneath his skin and bones.

A new thought hits me. 'Are you scared of yourself? Do you really want to kill people?'

'If I want them out of my way; yes, I do, Juliet.'

'Do you regret it?'

'*Regret-ah*.' He seems to taste the word, pondering its meaning. His fingers are drumming the top of my hand, which he still keeps pressed to his heart. 'You want me to be sorry. Makes it easier for you to be...' I hear him lick his lips close to my ear. '..Ah, a *savior*.'

I begin to lean away from him. 'I'm not saying that –'

'Bless me, sister, for I have sinned.' He rolls with me, not letting me create the distance between us that I wanted to make. His mouth presses directly to my ear, his jaw rubbing my cheek. 'Hail Mary, full of grace. Our Lord is with thee. Blessed art thou among women, and blessed is the fruit of thy womb, Jesus. Holy Mary, Mother of God, pray for us sinners, now and at the hour of our death, amen. Hail Mary, full of grace...'

'Stop saying that.'

'*Ave Maria, gratia plena...*'

'I'm not going to save you.'

He shifts his weight further, pressing his shoulder to mine, so that I'm pushed onto my back. My sleeping bag has slid down to my waist, leaving my chest uncovered but for my T-shirt, and he feels heavy on top of me, locking me between his arms, which he keeps on both sides of my head. His mouth shifts from my ear to my jaw, tracing slowly upwards. He's so warm, I think, vaguely wondering how he manages to keep his body temperature up when everything around us is near freezing level. When his lips reach my own, he pushes down and I quickly close my mouth, denying him the access he's seeking.

The Half Face laughs against my skin, a low, animalistic sound. He tangles his fingers into my hair and pulls my head back, a little harder than is comfortable. I recognize the warning to cooperate; and by now I know the pain that will follow if I don't give him what he wants.

I open my lips for him, just a little. His tongue slides over my bottom lip, exploring it. Then he pushes down harder and enters my mouth more deeply. He finds my tongue and caresses it, gently, almost playfully. Tiny jolts of electricity run through my body, like the pricks of a needle, surprising me so much that I don't do anything for a while, allowing him to kiss me, inside and on my lips. His right hand remains in my hair, keeping my head stuck to the ground. His other arm travels down, his fingers trailing down my cheek, further down across my throat, and then past my waist to the hem of my T-shirt, where he lifts the fabric and slips under it. His skin against mine is another shockingly intimate new experience, especially with his tongue still dancing around mine in a way that is getting very hard to resist.

He doesn't take a lot of time to explore my ticklish belly. His hand reaches up almost at once, wrapping itself around my left breast, his thumb already fiddling with the small border of lace at the top of my bra cup.

*If he takes it off, he'll find the chip.*

That frightening thought clears my head, but there's nothing I can do to stop him. I hear him groan, and he momentarily has mercy on my sore lips as he moves his head away from mine to position himself even more fully on top of me. His hips grind against mine. I make some kind of sound, I'm not even sure what I mean by it myself, but he must have taken it as encouragement, because in response he pushes down harder, and I feel something press between my legs.

The odd, feverish madness that possessed me a minute before dissolves at once, leaving me with a sense of danger and warning. I put my hands against his chest as he moves in to kiss me again, and somehow I have enough strength to actually make him stop for a second.

'I can't,' I whisper, shaking my head. 'I can't do it.'

'No?' His voice is husky, and even rawer than usual. 'Or *won't* you?'

I use the first lie that comes to mind. 'I can't because I'm on my period. I'm...I'm sorry.'

'Oh, *Ju-li-et!*' He lets go of my breast and wraps his hands around both sides of my head, resting his brow against mine and breathing heavily. 'Is this a game to you?'

'It's not my fault!'

'No.' He lets out another deep breath, and it runs over my face. 'I want you so much my skin could burst.'

'I would feel gross,' I whisper, my heart racing against my chest. I think he might actually be able to feel it.

'Sh sh, it's alright.' He kisses my brow, then my lips, then my cheek, and then lets me go, rolling off me with a heavy groan.

I lie still in the darkness, not daring to move, for fear

he will change his mind. Is this really happening? Did I just convince him to leave me alone without repercussion?

Before I can delight in my overwhelming sense of relief, he rolls back onto his side, his face to me. He doesn't climb on top of me again, but his hand finds his way back to my face, stroking my skin softly with one finger.

'You're beautiful to me even in the darkness, Juliet.'

I don't reply.

'Come here. Come. You'll get cold.' He gently pulls me back to him and I obey, allowing the warmth of his body to envelop me once again. He tucks up the sleeping bag all the way to my neck, but he pushes down the zipper, which is on his side, to change it from an isolated cocoon into one big blanket. I roll back to my usual position, my back to his chest, so that he won't get the chance to kiss me again.

As soon as I do it, I know I have made a mistake. He's under my T-shirt again, cupping my breast, and this time, he doesn't let go. His fingers move in slow, hypnotizing circles around my nipple, up and down and round and round.

'I'm going to make you want me until you're ready to have me,' he whispers in my neck.

Eventually I do manage to fall asleep, but until that time, his hand and his words make me feel cold and hot at the same time.

Just when I think that we've reached the end, because the food is gone, as well as the water, and I'm no longer able to make another step without falling over, the herders find us.

They're not the herders we are looking for, not Gansükh's people, but I don't think even the Half Face can feel much disappointment about that, right now. They are a small group, with a herd of about ten horses grazing on the hillside near a circular lake, and three *gers* resting on the grassy slope just above the shore. There are goats and a few sheep, and they have cooking fires inside their tents that almost make me melt from happiness.

They take us in with very little questions, offering us *airag* and *buuz*, the fried dumplings filled with meat, which taste of herbs and safety. Batzorig tells them a story of how we were robbed by our driver; how he stole our traveling gear as well as our car. It's true, in a way, and he's smart enough not to mention that the Half Face is carrying a gun beneath his coat.

The herders offer us a new escort, one of their own

experienced trackers on horseback. Yes, they have heard of Oyun and her daughter Tsend; they would gladly help us find our way back to their home. But once again, the Half Face shakes his head and utters the name of the other shaman: 'Gansükh.'

The mountain we are looking for, they tell us, is called Otgontenger. Without realizing it, we've slipped into the territory of the Khangai Mountains, and our destination is a week's ride away from here.

A week! My heart lifts up like a bird when I hear that. Just another seven days of hardship; it doesn't seem that much anymore. Almost bearable.

'One of them can escort us up to the foot of the mountain,' Batzorig's steady voice translates. 'They may know where to find the Reindeer Herders.'

I look at the Half Face expectantly. He ponders the offer, then shakes his head. 'We can find them on our own-*ah*.'

I think this journey is causing him to lose his mind more and more, even if he seems less violent as we progress. I don't tell him that – he's not yet that friendly.

The herders seem to be of the opinion that we are as stupid as I fear we are, but they don't comment on it anymore. Instead, they offer us provisions and horses.

The Half Face accepts.

They are small, bulky ponies, with short, cropped manes, muscled necks and friendly eyes. One of the herders, a pretty woman of middle age, gestures to a dark brown pony, smiling at me. The creature is already saddled: a piece of brown leather, two iron stirrups and a comfortable, high seat girdled around its belly, clearly designed to enable the rider to endure long treks through the steppe. There's a rope bridle wrapped around the horse's head, tied together with several knots.

I place my foot in one of the stirrups and let myself slide into the saddle. The width of the horse between my legs feels uncomfortable, straining my muscles. The woman smiles again and nods, then released her hold on the horse. I squeeze my calves into its side experimentally, and the horse steps forward at once. I'm a little shocked to find the creature moving beneath me, but after I get used to this strange sensation, I'm pleased to discover that the sturdy build of its back gives me a sense of stability and safety, rather than feeling like I'm balancing on a dangerously unstable construction.

Batzorig, of course, hops into the saddle with the ease of breathing. Even the Half Face manages to hold on to his grace as he mounts his pony, grabbing the reins in one hand with a determined fist. He rides up next to me, then turns his head to our interpreter.

'Tell them we are grateful,' he says, surprising me. 'Tell them that I'd give something in return, if I had more than the clothes on my back.'

Batzorig's eyebrows shoot up, but he translates the words into Mongolian without making a comment.

I stare at the Half Face, until he turns back to me and smiles. 'Would you have me be a thief, as well as a monster?'

'No,' I say quickly. 'That was very gallant of you.'

He licks his lips. *'Gallan-t.'*

'Like a knight.'

He throws his head back and laughs, long and hard. 'Yes, Juliet. A knight.'

Then he urges his horse forward, away from the small encampment. Batzorig and I follow him, he with a wave of his hand to the herders, who have all come out to watch us go. I stare at the Half Face's back, and wonder if this land is really shifting something inside of him.

# Chapter 15

## Blood

It is nearing twilight when the landscape of flat steppe changes. I hear a faint rush of water, like a stream is somewhere hidden beneath the rocks, or far away. To my right, the earth plunges down into a yawning hole, stretching as far as the mountains in the distance. It's a ravine, I realize, and a gigantic one. The two walls are made from solid rock, and when we draw closer, I can just briefly peer down into its depths. A river winds its way down below, wild and churning. I also notice that it's not just a sheer stone drop, but that the sides of the ravine are covered in woodland.

'We'll have to descend that path,' Batzorig says, striking fear into my heart at once.

'It's way too narrow! We could easily slip; what if...' I don't want to think about what would happen if my horse lost its balance.

'The horses know their way, Juliet,' he reassures me. 'Their legs are steady on these grounds. Trust them.'

I glance over at the Half Face, who hasn't said anything yet. Now he catches my gaze, and he gives me that lopsided grin that he likes so much. 'I can hold your hand, Julie. Here, let me support you.'

'No, I don't need that.' I prefer to keep my hands were they are, wrapped tightly around the reins of my pony, clamping down on them so hard that my knuckles are stretching the skin.

'Lean back in the saddle, and relax your belly,' Batzorig tells me. 'Don't use the reins, Juliet, they will be useless to you now. If you have to hold on, take the horse's mane.'

I nod, breathing out slowly to relax the muscles of my stomach. The interpreter is right, they feel as hard as a knot of metal wire, but once I force them to ease up, I feel a little steadier in the saddle. I watch with a growing sense of fear as Batzorig steers his pony to the edge of the ravine, where there's just a small trail leading down into a clutter of narrow birch trees. I follow him, letting the Half Face close the rear.

In reality, the path is not much steeper than some of the mountains we have already passed. It's not a broad trail, but broad enough for our ponies to walk down without much trouble. As long as we ride in single file, I figure we should be okay.

I lean back in my saddle as I'm told, and concentrate on the steady balance of my horse's back, rocking back and forth in the rhythm of its steps. I let the reins hang loosely around its neck, tangling my fingers in its prickly, cropped mane. It has just enough hair to hold on to.

After maybe fifteen minutes, the path changes. It expands, allowing two of the horses to ride next to each other, and the Half Face immediately joins my side. The downside is that the drop on his other side has become far steeper, and I'm not sure that I like the quality of the soil we're now treading on. It seems wetter, sucking in the horses' hooves with plopping sounds.

'Watch out, back there,' Batzorig suddenly says. He halts his horse, and we are forced to do the same.

'What is it *now*, Batty?'

'I don't like this much,' Batzorig mutters, nodding at a

particularly muddy part of the trail, just ahead of us. 'The earth is too soft from the rain, and the edge is too close. Better dismount.'

'Do we have to go this way?' I ask, my heart racing again as I slide off my pony. As soon as my feet touch the earth, I notice how my knees are trembling.

Batzorig hesitates. 'We could turn and avoid the ravine altogether, by finding a way around it.'

'How long would that take?' the Half Face asks.

'Days.'

He shakes his head. 'Then we go on. Julie – ahead of me.'

I obey without speaking, taking the reins in my hand and carefully stepping into Batzorig's footsteps as he tests his weight before taking the next step. His horse follows him with nervously twisting ears.

It happens so suddenly that I don't even have time to blink. I hear a low rumble, like a gigantic creature is waking up beneath our feet. When I whip my head around, the earth just behind me crumbles and falls away. I catch a glimpse of the Half Face. He looks utterly stunned. His bright eyes flash to mine, then he loses his grip, slips, and disappears over the edge of the ravine. Gone without a cry of fear.

I remain frozen in my place, my eyes wide open. He doesn't come back. I'm not sure what I'm seeing, and yet it is clearly there: the edge of the ravine, the deep, deep drop down, and the few thickets covering the steep walls of the empty space.

Batzorig is quicker of mind than I am. He sprints to the edge, leaving his horse. A moment later, he looks up at me. 'He's there!'

I look down. He's right. The Half Face hasn't dropped down into the river. There's a series of plateaus leading down to the river, and he's lying on his side on one of those. As I watch, he stirs, and I know that he's taken the plunge without dying.

'Can he climb up?' I ask.

'See, there's a trail leading down there,' Batzorig says in a trembling voice.

'Yes, but can he use it?'

'He can if he hasn't broken anything.'

'What if he has?'

The interpreter looks up and studies my face. 'I can go and get him.'

'Can...can you?' I'm hardly able to talk, that's how hard my heart is hammering against my chest. I've wished the Half Face dead many times since I first laid eyes on him, ever since that horrible day in Fallhallow, but now that he's down there, and I'm left up here with only one other human being, I'm suddenly terribly afraid.

'I'll take my horse,' Batzorig says. 'Four legs are better at climbing than two.'

'Wait!' If he goes down, and if he falls too, I'll be all by myself in this unknown, outstretched wilderness. That's not better at *all*, that's the worst I can think of.

'If we don't get him, he might die.' Batzorig says it quite plainly, and he sounds calm, despite the tremor in his voice. 'But he is not our friend. Take a second to think about this, Juliet.'

His eyes bore into mine, and I feel suddenly out of breath. What he is offering me is so tempting that it almost physically hurts. But it's also terrible, because it would mean letting a human being die, right in front of my eyes.

Again, just like when my captor pushed the gun into my hand and offered me his head, I feel a little black creature licking on the inside of my brain; enticing me to do the worst I've got, to take an eye for an eye – one life for the dozens of Fallhallow National Bank.

'But I'm *not* Black,' I say aloud, to convince myself that the statement is true. 'I'm *not* him, I *won't* be, I *can't* be, I'll *never* be!'

'Stay up here.' Batzorig retrieves his horse, mounts it, and begins to descend, down the dangerously steep slope leading down to the first plateau.

'Stay?' I repeat. I'm not going to wait up here, not on my own. I get off my horse and leave it there, not really caring if it runs off or not. Batzorig may be a natural horseman, but I'm not so sure that I trust my pony to make its way down without falling.

I make my way to the first plateau by the time Batzorig has steered his horse down to the second, where the thickets seem to cling to the soil in a frightful attempt not to fall off. The drop would be steep and fast. The river is directly below us, I realize, as I clamber to the edge and begin my second descent. It's not so far down that I can't make out the rush of dark, splashing water, angrily beating against everything that dares to get in its way.

The sight of that river makes me halt without realizing it, my breath coming out in quick, shallow huffs. Batzorig reaches the Half Face, who is conscious, even if he looks mildly confused.

'You need my horse,' the interpreter says. I can just hear him above the roar of the water.

The Half Face shakes his head. He accepts Batzorig's

hand as he offers it to help him to his feet. He staggers; for a moment I'm convinced that he is going to fall down after all, but he regains his balance and nods to Batzorig, a brief offer of thanks.

'Hold on to the horse's neck; grab his mane,' the interpreter tells my captor. 'He's stable, he'll hold us both. And he can climb better than you.'

They begin to make a steady way up, and I'm already breathing out deeply, relief calming down my racing heart. When they reach a part where the rock face closes them in on both sides, so that the path turns into a narrow trail, Batzorig halts. The Half Face grabs a hand full of thorny branches and heaves himself up, past the neck of the horse, to make his way up first.

Batzorig waits a while to let my captor get a head start, then moves to follow. There's a weird noise filling the air. First I ignore it, but after a few moments, I suddenly can't block it out anymore, and I look around to find the source of it.

It's a very low, very deep kind of sound. It's almost a moan, but I'm pretty sure that it can't be made by any kind of animal that I've ever heard of. I look down again. The Half Face has reached the second plateau, where he is safe. He stretches his legs and straightens up, shooting a look my way.

I look past him, to the side of the plateau where Batzorig is still steadily ascending. The thorn bushes are all strangely leaning to the side, tilted towards the river. I blink. Did the ground look that way when we got here?

Suddenly, I *do* realize what the noise is. My heart stops; then starts again at a nauseating speed.

'Batzorig! Batzorig! Look out!' I shout, bringing my hands to my mouth in an attempt to amplify the sound. 'It's moving!' My voice reaches him over the roar of the river and he looks up, but doesn't spot the danger. All I can do is watch. I shout myself hoarse as the earth inevitably gives in to the weight of a man on a horse. It happens at a snail's pace at first, almost like watching a movie in slow-motion. But then the soil suddenly shifts, crashing down with the speed of striking lightning, and my friend tumbles down into the depth.

I cry out his name, scrambling over the bushes and the thickets to climb down the same precarious path he has taken minutes before. When I reach the plateau where the Half Face is looking on in stunned silence, I see a part of the river rushing wildly below us.

The Half Face grabs my arm as I run to the bank and stops me before I can teeter off the edge as well.

'There.' He points.

I watch as an icy cold terror washes over me, spreading its chills all through my body. The man and the horse have been flung at least a hundred meters downstream. To my relief, I notice that the horse is holding up its head above the surface, even if just barely, in a desperate attempt not to drown. It's swimming – fighting to reach the shore. I spot Batzorig only seconds later. He's also alive; at least, his arms are wrapped around the horse's neck and he's not letting go, so I think he must be. His leg is still stuck in one of the stirrups, bent awkwardly upward in an angle that can't be humanly possible under normal circumstances.

I push that thought from my mind as I pull myself from the Half Face's grip and slide down the last meters to the edge of the river, then run up to the place where the horse is struggling to get out of the water.

The poor beast is panting heavily, its flanks rising and falling, its nostrils flaring and its eyes rolling wildly up, so I can clearly see the white of its eyeballs. As soon as its legs touch solid ground, it tumbles down. There's blood in its mouth, spilling out rapidly.

I ignore it, because Batzorig just disappeared beneath the horse, and I really think I heard something snap loudly. Something that sounded like bone.

'Help me!' I cry, and the Half Face is suddenly next to me, putting his weight into the horse to push it aside. The horse makes a strange sound; a low groan that I didn't even know horses could make.

Batzorig's torso appears. His head limply lolls to the left, but his eyelids flutter, which tells me he is alive still. The horse can't or won't budge another inch, which leaves Batzorig's legs still trapped underneath the animal's weight. It's alright, I tell myself, even though I vaguely understand that the crushing I heard earlier must be from his bones. We can sort that out later. We can fix him up.

I lower myself to him and gently rest my hands on his shoulders.

He shrieks, suddenly and loudly, making me jump and whimper with fright. 'What did I do? How could that hurt?'

The interpreter doesn't answer. His eyes roll up, looking past me to an invisible point, like a man suffering from a heavy fever.

'But we have to get you away from the horse, so we can fix you after that,' I explain desperately. There's blood coming from his mouth too, just like from the horse. 'Batzorig...'

He is making strange, wet, choking noises. After a moment, I realize that he is crying in agony, and all of a sudden I feel like my head just shatters. I want to fix him, help him, save him, make sure that the broken body that I see before me gets sorted out the way it should be, but whatever I do with my frantically moving hands, it doesn't seem to make a difference.

'I'm sorry,' I sob, 'I'm trying, I'm trying, but I don't know what to do –'

'Julie, move back.'

As I look over my shoulder, I let out another great sob when I see the Half Face standing behind me with his gun drawn. 'Please, fix him,' I whisper, even though a part of me knows what he is going to do. 'I can't find the right way, so you fix him. Fix him!'

'Move.' He grabs my shoulder and pulls me aside. I tumble to the left, but not far.

'Don't,' I say, looking at the gun, which he is now pointing at the horse.

The gunshot resonates across the rush of the water below us. The horse jerks violently, just once, then its muscled neck relaxes and its head drops to the ground with a sickening thud.

'Right in the head. Didn't even feel it.' The Half Face's

voice is softer than usual.

Batzorig looks scared when the Half Face points the gun back at him.

'He's not a horse!' I cry, struggling to get to my feet, even though all my limbs have turned to jelly. 'That's my friend! Please, oh, please, please, don't hurt him, just fix him, he can get better, please, just help him.'

'He's never going to get better.'

I stare at him, then back at Batzorig, whose face seems to have drained of all blood. His eyes are strangely bulging, rolling back in his sockets like he's a scared animal. I fight my impulse to gag.

This shot appears to be even louder and harsher than the one before. It pierces my eardrums. The Half Face is a precise shot. He fired the bullet exactly between Batzorig's eyes. Now there's a third hole in his skull, like a new eye. The blood gushing out of it is thick, almost like syrup. I can't hold it in anymore and empty my stomach on the ground. It's disgusting and sour. I make gagging sounds, which turn into hoarse, deep roars. I'm not shouting any words – I'm beyond words, and this is an animal's anguish, not Juliet's.

'Get up.'

It takes minutes for me to even make out the Half

Face's voice. I shake my head wildly, refusing to let go of Batzorig, whom I've started to cradle in my crouched position.

'Juliet! Let go of the corpse-*ah*.'

It's that word, more than his command, that shakes me from my state of feverish shock. My grip slackens, and I feel two hands pulling me backwards. I still can't use my legs, so I remain on the ground, staring at the sight before me. The man and the horse are both twisted in the oddest of ways, their bones smashed and broken by their long fall. The sleeves of my T-shirt stick to my wrists. I look at them. I'm covered in blood, up to my elbows.

A warm body presses into me from behind, steadying my back, and the Half Face's cheek leans against mine. 'There is *nothing* you can do for him.'

'He came down to save you.' I am barely audible, still sobbing.

'Yes.'

'He should have let you die there.'

He is quiet for a moment, then his warmth disappears from my back. I don't care. I stay where I am, not allowing my eyes to wander away from Batzorig. The Half Face isn't worth anything, as far as I'm concerned now – not when this man gave his life in an attempt to save his sorry ass.

My captor walks around the bodies, crouching down opposite them. He picks up something from the ground, something that must have fallen out of Batzorig's pockets.

'What is this?' he asks, holding up a small, silver coin between his fingers.

'I don't know,' I whisper, my voice still thick from tears. What I mean to say is that I don't care, because I vaguely register that it is another chip he is holding, and that Batzorig must have carried it with him all along. Another tracker. The Mongolian Police will know exactly where we are.

And yet, right now, it is completely unimportant, because my friend is a broken, dead mess on the ground.

I reach out a shaking, blood-covered hand and touch Batzorig's eyelids, trying to shut them to hide those terrible, lightless pupils. It doesn't work. His whole body has turned stiff.

'Oh, God,' I whisper. I crumble like a brittle, dry plant, covering my head with my arms.

The Half Face leaves me like this for a while, as he goes off. I don't really know what he's doing – maybe checking on the horses, or making sure that the rest of the path is safe to walk on. When he comes back, he hooks his hands underneath my arms and lifts me up without comment. I stagger, struggling to keep my balance on my two feet, and after a few seconds he drags me away from Batzorig.

'Wait,' I stammer, numbed by pain. All of this feels so unreal. 'We can't just leave him here.'

'We *are* leaving him here.'

'No. No, that's not right!'

'And I'm not here to be right-*ah*.' He gives me another push, and I stumble forward, up the slippery path to the relative safety of the first plateau. I look up. It's such a steep climb, and I feel sick to my core. How am I going to get all the way up there again, and mount my horse like nothing has happened? All I want is to sink down again, maybe find a little shelter in the shadow of a jutting boulder, and wait out the night.

The Half Face takes my arm again. This time he doesn't push, or pull, or squeeze me. He gently helps me up, urging me to put one foot in front of the other, showing me where to direct my next step, which thickets I should grab to keep my balance. I listen to his voice directing me, obeying his orders. It's easier this way, really. He gives me a purpose, a lifeline to cling to, and that's all that matters now.

At some point, we reach the place where we have left the horses. He gathers the reins in his one hand, keeping the fingers of his other hand around my lower arm. I'm relieved to see that he doesn't steer us to the muddy path that made Batzorig hesitate; instead, we go all the way up again. Somewhere halfway, the Half Face pauses to let me catch my breath, and then he gets me on my pony. I lean forward without a word, burying my face in its mane, allowing it to bring me back to the top of the ravine, where the steppe catches us and embraces us with its vastness like the arms of a mother.

The Half Face mounts too, and we ride. I don't know for how long, I don't care where to. For once, I'm not scared when the sun dips below the horizon and dark settles over the land. It's a comforting darkness, this time. Like a thick blanket, blocking the rest of the world from my mind. As long as I can't see, I don't have to think about the pain that I'm feeling, tearing my chest apart.

'Julie,' the Half Face's voice murmurs, drifting towards me after hours of silence. 'Look up.'

I open my eyes and look. The sky is a deep, pitch-black ocean, yet it's never been so light. After a second I realize that what I'm looking at is a sea of stars, scattered all over the firmament, like seeds thrown out over a barren field. They cluster together and break apart in millions of patterns. I've never seen so many stars. I couldn't even have imagined it.

'Beau-ti-ful-*ah*.'

Yes, it is beautiful. I try to take in every individual bulb of light, craning my neck. It's impossible; as soon as I shift my gaze, I lose count and have to start over. There are stars that stand out clearly, looking so close that it's like I only need to reach out to pluck them from the sky, and others that seem to avoid my eyes in little dances, only ever visible on the edge of my vision.

There are some constellations that I think I recognize – the Big Dipper and Ursa Major. I remember them from my early school days, drawing the dots of the stars on a piece of paper, connecting them with yellow lines. *That's what I should teach the children*, I catch myself thinking; *the rotation of the world and how many stars are in the sky if you turn off the lights of a city.*

And I could tell them about the taste of *airag* and *buuz*. I imagine myself standing in front of a breathless group as I describe the drums of the two shaman women, hitting the rhythm of an excited heart on a cardboard box, shoving aside chairs and tables to let them whirl and dance around the room with colored feathers and ribbons adorning their clothes.

That's what I will do, I decide. After I survive this

journey. If I survive it at all.

When the Half Face halts our horses and pitches our single tent, I forget about my little surge of optimism and sink back into my grief for Batzorig. It's easy to blame the Half Face for his death, but when he wraps his two arms around me in an embrace that is more soothing than lustful, I discover that it is even easier to surrender to his comfort.

# Chapter 16

## Never had so little to lose

'What are we going to do now?' I ask, when my eyes have cried too much to shed more tears without aching, and my throat feels raw. 'Even if we ever find Gansükh, we have no one to translate for us.'

I'm still in his arms. He's stroking my hair slowly. It almost feels normal; just a young couple in an unusual place, faced with the sudden harsh reality of the termination of life. The fact that he is the only living, breathing human for miles around makes it so much easier to stay this way.

'This is not the reason you grieve for him,' the Half Face mutters.

'No, but it is the reason I worry.'

'No, it is not-*ah*. You worry, Julie, because you have been betrayed and deserted.'

I shake my head. 'How have I been betrayed?'

He brings his lips close to my ear. I feel the stubbles on his jaw brush against the skin of my face, but I don't move – my head is too heavy, too painful. 'Because he left you. *All. Alone.* With me.'

'Oh, get over yourself!' I sit up straight, untangling myself from his arms in one angry motion. It's hard to tell where this sudden rage is coming from; a minute ago I felt nothing but a numb bleakness, but now that it's here, I don't want to let go of it. It's so much better than the cold chill of mourning. 'Do you really think I still care about your stupid threats and your stupid way of talking? You think that's somehow intimidating? Or is it artistic? Everybody can talk like that! "Give me the gun-*ah*! Let's have things es-ca-*late*, why so *serious*?!"' I pause to take a deep breath, then carry on in a rush: 'You're just a scarred man with a painted head and a sexual frustration. Well, cry me a river! Nobody gets through life unscathed, and you're not the frigging epitome of suffering. My God, it's like you've emerged from an angsty teenage novel, and how old are you anyway? Thirty?' I stare at him, my eyes ablaze.

He remains still for a couple of seconds; moments in which I can count each of my erratic heartbeats. Then he grabs the flashlight and turns it on with a sudden movement, almost blinding me.

'You are,' he says, making the light dance over my face, 'a hurtful person. Did anyone tell you that?'

'Oh, did it *hurt*? Try having your air cut off for speaking out of turn! Try having a grown man grab you so hard you have bruises because you're trying not to get kidnapped – oh, try getting dragged all over Mongolia as a hostage with a gun habitually shoved into your face, and *then* drag up the guts to tell me that *I* have hurt YOU!'

'Try this!' His hand shoots toward me, grabbing me roughly by the collar of my sweater, pulling me towards him with an angry jerk. 'Try having a hissing voice in your head telling me to break your neck, that I now have to ignore!'

'Oh, you'd better ignore it.' Despite my angry words, I feel myself shudder to my core. 'Because I'm your Madonna, right?'

He stares at me, his face close to mine and his fist under my chin, still clutching my sweater tightly. Finally, he lets me go. 'Yes. You have never talked like this before,' he adds, after a while.

I crawl away from him and curl my legs under me, staring at him in the light of the flashlight. 'Well, I've never had so little to lose.'

We look at each other for a while, both silent. I wonder if he gets it. If there maybe is a part of him that understands that things have gone too far, and that the best we can hope for now is damage control. When he doesn't speak, I finally sigh deeply.

'We have no food. We have no water left. We don't really know where we are and even if we did, we only have each other to rely on, and no one to translate for us. This is bad, Half Face. This is the worst that could have happened. You realize this, don't you?'

'And yet we are close to the mountain.'

I do my best to ignore a new hot surge of anger. 'Look. I'm going to be on the lookout for a group of herders from now on. I don't care how close we are to the mountain; our best chance of survival is another *ger*. We might be lucky, we might find someone tomorrow. If...*when* we do...I'm going to ask them to help us get back to Ulaanbaatar. I won't tell them who you are, don't even worry about that. Heck, I don't even know *how* I'd tell them, if I wanted to.

But this...' I gesture to the wilderness around us, outside our tent. 'This has escalated too much. I'm not willing to die here, Half Face. Not for you! Not for anyone.'

He just shakes his head. 'I can't let you go and walk off, Julie. I need you.'

'I know what you need. It's not this. It's not...starving out in the cold in this empty land. I promise you.' As soon as I say those last words, my anger floods away, my voice breaks and I'm back on the verge of tears. 'It's *help* you need, Half Face. Back home, back in the courtroom. That's where it's gonna start; not out here. That's your road to redemption. Why can't you just see that?'

'Mmm. And I bet you will testify against me once again, little Julie. How do you think I would app-re-ci-ate that?'

I'm struck by a sudden wave of inspiration. 'Maybe I don't have to be against you,' I tell him quietly. 'I could tell everyone how much you want to free yourself. That I have grown to see a better man in you. After all, you haven't hit me for a while now. You even helped Batzorig...in a way. Maybe we're both right – maybe this place is doing something for you. The quiet. The space. The healing. I can tell them that...It would count for something.'

'And yet, I would be locked away for decades. Maybe

even a lifetime.'

'Maybe that wouldn't be the worst for you,' I say, automatically expecting him to lunge forward, his hands squeezing my arms, or his fingers wrapping around my throat in a death grip. To my surprise, he only leans in on me, his brow almost touching mine. I feel his warm breath tingle on my skin.

'And what would I do *all* that time without my Julie, huh?'

'Take...take that time to figure it all out,' I say. Could it be that he is actually considering my words? My heart starts beating faster. Perhaps all he needs is someone to save him, after all. Perhaps I *could* be the one. 'Drag out every scrap of goodness you can find inside of you and use it to better yourself.'

'And you'll be waiting for me once I walk out a free man?' he murmurs. I hear a hint of irony in his voice.

My spirits drop. 'I don't think I can do that.'

'You see, Jools, I don't think I have to go through all that *trou*-ble, when I have you *right here,*' he chuckles, burying his face in my hair.

The brief spell of optimism leaves me as rapidly as it came. There is no way to save him, I realize somberly. And

I shouldn't even try. Instead, I must focus on saving myself.

# Chapter 17

## The Edge

Sometimes, things end gradually. They meander to an end, where they dry up, or burn out. I have lost friendships this way, and in hindsight, I guess this is how Chris and I ended. Sometimes, there's just nothing left.

Other times, things stop abruptly, the way a gunshot stops a life. I can't tell what ending I had imagined for this terrible journey; I think I had started to believe that it would just go on forever, like the steppe we were trying to cross, and that any kind of ending would simply keep skipping ahead of us, just as that terrible horse-headed mountain.

The thing about gradual endings is that you can always see it coming, whether you're looking forward to it or not. The quick ending, the bullet shot, gets you like a thunderbolt. It's like finding yourself on the edge of an abyss, and falling down, before you even have time to be scared.

On that last morning, we ride out, closer to the mountain than ever. It still looks distant to me, but the Half Face is happy, whistling a tune through his teeth. The silence and the magnitude of the land seem to have a calming effect on him. My last yellow-green bruises have all faded. Perhaps what is really calming him is the lack of other people, I think, as I let myself be rocked by the rhythm of the horse. There's no one left to shout at now. Well, of course, there's me. Now that it's day again, I wonder what last night's brave words really meant. Can I simply ride off and hand him over to his own insane quest? Do I dare? Is it even wise?

The truth is, I *don't* dare. Even if a part of me wants to tuck on the reins, turn my pony around and canter off before he can realize what I have done, it won't guarantee my safety at all.

Personally, I'm beginning to feel that the impressive landscape is getting repetitively dull; the mountains, the lakes, the occasional patches of trees. Even the night skies, the millions of stars. I guess this means a person can get used to anything.

'Julie, sing with me!' the Half Face says, breaking my contemplative silence. I feel annoyed; the silence was alright by me; a bubble of relative safety, and I liked it in there.

'I don't know any songs,' I tell him.

He laughs. 'Don't be a liar.'

'I really don't know what to sing.'

'Sing anything.' He slows down his horse and falls into step with me, giving me his lopsided grin, and even a wink. 'I will give you ten points, just for trying. Come on, *Ju*-lie, defy the silence a little. The steppe will forget the sound of your voice soon enough-*ah*.'

I close my eyes and open my mouth. The words are just the first that pop up in my mind; an old nursery rhyme. I don't even know what it's about, I've never known.

*'If you sing loud and clear, she will hear, she will hear*
*If you sing clear and loud, call her out, call her out*
*If it is time to rise, up to Christ, up to Christ*
*she will lift your soul to paradise.'*

When I'm done, I notice him looking at me curiously. I

quickly shift my gaze ahead of me, where the hills are soggy-brown rather than green now. There's a strange noise in the air; a little too distant to make out, but it bothers me. The Half Face doesn't notice it yet, or else he ignores it, because he just keeps staring at me. He reaches out a hand and takes mine, his fingers enveloping me hard enough that I can't pull back.

A white dot breaks the greenish-brown hue on the slope of the hill ahead. Another one quickly follows after that, and then another one.

'You sing like a catholic school girl,' the Half Face says. As if this is somehow a good thing. I hear the lust in his raw voice.

'Look,' I say.

'Oh, I *am*, Julie. I see everything. I want to touch toni –'

'No. *Look.*'

The white dots have just turned into *gers*. Of course they are, what else could possibly be out here that looks so lovely that it makes my heart ache? And spilling down the hill, riding towards us, is a small party on horseback. I can make out their colorful garments long before I see their faces.

The Half Face doesn't say much once we are surrounded by the Mongolian riders. He must be a little relieved, I think, looking at his face. He displays no emotions, but I know he is as hungry as I am, and thirsty too.

They ask us questions that neither of us can understand.

'Do you speak English?' I try pleadingly. 'Just a little would be enough.'

'English.' It's a young woman with a broad, pretty face. Her eyes seem to pop out, that's how much light she catches in them. Her hair is pulled back in an intricate pattern of braids, a more complex version of the braid Tsend had made for me. She wears a bright red tunic, a blue sash and rides a jet-black pony without the comfort of a saddle. She smiles at me and repeats the word: 'English. Me.'

'Oh, God,' I whisper, relief spilling over me like an enormous tidal wave. 'Thank you. Please, please help us. We're starving, we're lost. We need to get to Ulaa –'

'Gansükh,' the Half Face interrupts me sharply. He raises a hand and jabs the air with it, pointing at the mountain. 'We. Need. The. Shaman.'

'No,' I say, shaking my head. 'We need to get to Ulaanbaatar. The city. Please?'

The girl seems confused by our flurry of contradicting words, and she mutters something to her companions, who all look at us, look back at the mountain, and begin to chatter excitedly. After a while, she holds up her hands and shouts something, her voice quite shrill when she raises it. The rest falls silent.

She looks at me again, smiling, and points at herself. 'I am Narantsuyaa.'

'I'm Juliet.'

'You lost?'

'Yes,' I say with a shuddering breath, suddenly feeling my eyes burn. 'We're very lost.'

'You want city. Ulaanbaatar.'

'I do. He doesn't. He wants to find the shaman Gansükh.'

'Gansükh. Yes. Up in mountain.'

'Yes. But can you help us?'

'Food. Drink. Home.' The girl nods. 'You follow, we help.'

I'm so relieved that I'm a little dizzy, but the Half Face rides up to me until he's so close that our knees are touching. 'Food and drink is all fine, but they are not taking you home just yet.'

'She just means shelter. Like a *ger*,' I say wearily. 'And

anyway, what choice do we have? If we leave now, we die.'

At least he can't seem to find any argument against that. If it's not his conscience, after glancing at my bone-weary and drooping face, then it must be his growling stomach. The entire party turns around and marches us back up the hill, as if they are a special welcoming committee. Like they have ridden out just to meet us, and...

I edge my horse closer to the girl, who gives me another smile.

'Naratsuyaa,' I mutter. 'How much English do you know?'

She holds up her hand, thumb and index finger indicating a measurement. 'Small bit,' she says, then drops her voice to a whisper. 'Police in *ger*, Juliet. Don't look scared.'

But that's impossible. At first, I think I have simply misunderstood her, and then I believe that she didn't know that she made a mistake. Maybe she meant to say please or ease or sleep in the *ger*. I stare at her and mouth the word, articulating as well as I can. 'Po-lice?'

She nods.

Oh, God. My hands suddenly turn soaking wet and cold, my throat tightens up. The *gers* are only a little ways away now. I can already see the colorful little flags attached to the roofs. They're fluttering in the wind as if they're beckoning us especially.

I look at the Half Face again. He hasn't heard a word we just said, and keeps throwing glances at the mountain.

'Do I have to do anything?'

'Nothing, Juliet.'

When we halt in front of the first *ger*, a larger one than I have ever seen before, my mouth is so dry that it's as though I have eaten sand. The Half Face dismounts quickly and gracefully. I need a while longer to untangle my feet from the stirrups, and by the time I've finally managed to move my legs, I feel his arms closing around my waist as he gently lifts me down from the horse.

I am shaking all over.

'What is it?' he asks.

'Nothing,' I whisper. 'I'm just so hungry.'

'You can rest now, Julie.' He turns me around in his arms and I stare up at his face, so close to mine. His body is warm. I've turned cold as ice. When he leans forward to kiss me, I don't flinch or move. His lips brush mine, open them, and the tip of his tongue slips into my mouth. I press my lips to his, just for the duration of a heartbeat, and then I step back. He has his eyes still closed, so he doesn't see what I see. How the tent flap of the *ger* opens noiselessly and four, five, ten people slip out, dressed in bulletproof vests.

'Half Face,' I say, just before he opens his eyes and two police officers reach out to grab him and take him in a headlock. 'Don't fight.'

He does fight, of course. I doubt he even heard me. His eyes snap open and stare at me, bulging. I can see the white of his eyeballs, and the anger that fills him once he realizes what is going on. Despite the strong hold of the police officers, he kicks and wrestles and roars. Someone pulls me away from the scene, away from the flailing hands and legs. I look on, completely mute. My heart is racing.

They lock his wrists in metal cuffs and they force him to the ground. Two men drop down on him with full force. All I can think of is how much that must hurt. Not only physically, but how it will destroy his pride.

His roar turns into a single word, yelled over and over again. 'Juliet! Juliet! JULIET!'

I try not to hear it. Behind the *ger* is a large, bulky thing. I focus on that, and realize that what I'm looking at is a helicopter. It must have made the noise that I was hearing earlier. I can't believe I didn't even recognize the sound of an engine. Have I grown so numb, or have the sounds of the steppe simply filtered out all the other sounds from my memory?

'JULIET! JULIET! JU-LI-ET!'

In the turmoil, I stand frozen and confused. The Half Face's voice penetrates both my body and my mind, even when I press my hands to my ears in a desperate attempt to block him out.

A female police officer grabs my shoulders. Automatically, I jump, then cringe, expecting the Half Face to haul me away, lock me in his arms again and press his gun to my head.

'No fear,' the woman says, realizing her mistake. She lets me go and points at the helicopter instead. 'Home.'

That single word. It carries enough power to break through my paralysis. Because I know what *that* means. It's the best thing I have heard in all these long days.

'What will happen to him?' I ask, just as the Half Face stops calling my name and the silence shocks me almost as much as his cries.

The officer shakes her head again. 'No fear,' she repeats, and this time I don't shrink back as she guides me to the helicopter, helping me to climb in. She buckles the safety belt for me. I lean back in the seat.

Even so, I expect the Half Face to suddenly break free of his captivity, to take me back into the confinement of his arms. This fear is still with me by the time the engine starts growling, when the door is closed and my body vibrates from the force with which the aircraft rises up. Only when I cast a glance out of the window and notice that we're already ten meters above the ground, do I suddenly realize the truth of the matter. Yesterday, we were on the edge, and the fall looked too steep to handle. Today, we're over it, and the fall is the best thing in the world.

Because even the Half Face can't fly. This terrible, shaking, noisy aircraft is giving me what no horse or shaman could do for me, what Batzorig tried to tell me but failed to do so, before his life was terminated.

I am free.

# Chapter 18

## Free

I'm back in another hotel in Ulaanbaatar. It's not the same as the one the Half Face took me to before. That one was impoverished, clammy, and small. This is a real, grand place, with marble pillars in the lobby and cushioned seats and thickly carpeted floors. But the city around it is just as run-down as before, and a part of me feels like I never even left.

They wanted to stay with me all night. A female police officer even offered to share my room. I told them not to bother. I don't mind being alone. I relish the sensation of moving around, sitting, standing, eating, staring or even singing aloud without eyes that follow me, take me in, measure me up and contemplate how I am doing. I've had enough of that to last me a lifetime.

Before they let me rest, they wanted to take my statement, so they brought me to a square, gray building that I figured was the police department of Ulaanbaatar. Someone put a cup of steaming tea into my hands, and then they asked me questions. There was a new interpreter, a young man with bright eyes and a smile tugging at the corner of his mouth. His accent was American, not the heavy, harsh tone that Batzorig used.

I told them what I could, almost without faltering. I described our landing at the airport, how he used his gun to ensure that not even the Mongolian police officers would try and end the situation. I told them, without embarrassment, that I kept the chip in my bra all this time, and I learned that is how they'd been tracking us. The police found Oyun and Tsend's *ger* only days after we had left. Tsend had told them everything she had gathered from me, and pointed the officers in the direction of the horse-headed mountain. Next, they found the herders, and traveled past the ravine.

I told them what happened to Batzorig. I told them where they could find his body. I turned my face away and choked a little. They gave me another cup of tea.

As soon as they showed me my phone, wrapped in a plastic bag, I remembered how the Half Face had taken it from me. I tried to grab it, but they wouldn't let me have it. They wanted to use it as evidence. I just wanted to use it to make a phone call, but after a moment, I realized that it wouldn't have a signal here anyway, so I gave up and let them keep it.

They brought me to a landline phone, helped me punch in a complicated arrangement of numbers, and then left me alone as I pressed the receiver to my ear. For some reason, my heart was racing and my hands were all clammy.

The phone rang three times before someone on the other end answered it.

'Hello?' It was a familiar, female voice.

'Mom,' I said.

There was a deep silence on the other end. I heard someone breathing hard, and I had to swallow something thick clogging up my throat.

'Julie,' my mother said after a while, her voice shaking. 'Are you there?'

'Yes, mom,' I whispered. 'It's me. I'm here.'

'God. Oh, God. Oh, Juliet, are you – does this mean – tell me if –'

I laughed and suddenly I was also crying. 'I'm alright. I'm with the police. They got him, mom. I'm coming home.'

'When?'

'There's a flight leaving tomorrow. I'll see you soon – you...you will pick me up, right?'

I heard her shout something that sounded like a muffled curse. 'Are you mad? Of course I'm coming – Oh, Julie, I'm so relieved I can't speak!'

'Don't,' I said, feeling a rush of cold. 'Just call me Juliet.'

'I don't –'

'Please.'

'Okay, Juliet. You're alright, are you? He didn't...did he?'

'I'm not even hurt a bit,' I said, though I might have been lying a little there. It was true that my bruises were gone and that he never really forced himself on me. But that didn't mean that I was not beaten and broken. I wouldn't tell mom this, of course. She deserved to be happy. Hell, I wanted to be happy.

After I'd hung up, they took me back to the hotel and

left me alone, with the promise that I will be picked up tomorrow morning, that they will escort me to the airport and get me on my flight back home. There will be a police attendant with me the entire way. I agreed. It made me feel safe. There's just one thing I needed to know.

'He won't be on the same flight, will he?'

'He is still in custody for now,' the young interpreter translated. 'He won't be flown back until we've got all clearances from the Fallhallow Police Force.'

Now, I'm trying to imagine the Half Face in a tiny cell, with only a thin mattress to sleep on. Is he raging right now, throwing himself against the door, still shouting my name? The thought of that makes my blood turn to ice. Maybe he's sitting in a corner, lethargy washing out the liveliness on his painted face. I wonder if he's really that sorry that things ended this way. There must be a part of him that feels a little relieved. He didn't fool me completely. He knew, just as well as I did, that the journey was a hopeless one. I was just better at recognizing it.

As soon as I'm left in my hotel room and the police are gone, I sink down on the king-sized bed. I think about sleeping, but in all honesty, my mind is a restless whirl. So I get off the bed again and head for the bathroom, which is twice the size of the bathroom where I had locked myself up. There's absolutely no reason for me to lock the door now, yet I still do it, feeling better knowing that nobody can sneak up on me.

I turn on the shower to the max, allowing the hot water vapor to fill the entire bathroom, steaming up the mirror. I kick off my clothes and stand under the downpour of water until I feel like I have soaked up every bit of warmth that my body can contain. Then I grab the hotel shampoo and use the entire bottle on my hair, rubbing it in as hard as I can. I don't rinse it out until I have taken an unwrapped toothbrush and brushed my mouth for at least five minutes, rinsing my mouth twice. Only after I have done all of that, and have scrubbed my body up and down with a pink sponge, I begin to feel clean.

Reluctantly, I put my clothes back on. They still smell like the steppe. I should have asked the police for new things to wear. Well, it won't be too long this time. Once I'm home, I will throw these items out or burn them, whichever works best. I lose myself in a fantasy where we ceremoniously throw the long sleeved T-shirt, the vest and the waterproof jacket on a pile of wood, igniting them in a bonfire. We could dance and chant around the flames in joy, moving like the shaman women. Yes, that would be nice, I think, and I smile.

There's a knock on my door. I freeze for a second, immediately alarmed. I open the door to a crack and peer out. It's just a lady of the hotel, pulling a trolley.

'Your dinner,' she says. This is the hotel where businessmen come to when they are flown out to Ulaanbaatar, and all the staff speak English. That's another relief. 'Did you want to have it in the dining room, miss?'

'No,' I say, shaking my head. I step back and open the door completely, feeling a bit silly now. 'This is perfect, thank you.'

She smiles and pulls the trolley to the middle of my room. It's laden with all kinds of food and the smell makes my belly grumble. I recognize the spiced dumplings and a bottle of *airag*, but there's also a tray full of steamed vegetables, a chicken salad, bowls of rice and fish, a soup terrine and slices of buttered bread.

'Can I get you anything else, miss?'

'No, thank you – or, actually...This is a little weird, but could I get some fresh clothes? These are...Well, I don't like them.'

She looks me up and down for a moment, then nods. 'I get that. I'll see what I can do for you.'

For the next half hour, I busy myself with polishing off every dish on the trolley, stuffing slices of bread in my mouth along with pieces of chicken, eating the dumplings together with the fish. I don't care, I'm not picky, I just want to feel warm and satisfied again. The only thing that I don't touch is the *airag*. I finish a bottle of orange juice instead.

When I'm done and the woman comes to take the trolley away, she's carrying a bundle of clothes.

'From the police,' she says, handing me the garments, and then puts something else in my hands, giving me a wink. 'And this is on the house.'

It's a large box, filled with chocolates. I'm so moved that I could almost weep.

I make tea with the water boiler and the tea bags that are available in the room, change into the fresh pair of jeans and the knitted sweater, and lie on the bed with the TV on, eating as many chocolates as I can after gobbling down most of my dinner.

Flipping through the channels doesn't bring up anything interesting. Most of them are in Mongolian anyway, and I don't feel like watching CNN. There are a couple of DVDs on the shelf. I rummage through them, eventually picking Bridget Jones' Diary, and I watch it with the most content feeling I've ever experienced. Tomorrow, I'll go home. Right now, I'm on my own, which is so incredibly liberating that the silence around me when the movie is finished feels like an ointment to my soul.

On impulse, I get up, open my door and step out into the corridor. There's nobody here but me. I walk up to a staircase, turn back and walk the other way, swinging my arms wildly. It's like I can *feel* the absence of the Half Face in the air. When I hear an unexpected sound I freeze, whipping my head the other way, but it's just another hotel guest at the end of the corridor, pulling out his key and entering his room without even sparing me a glance.

I laugh out loud.

No one is watching me. No one is preying on me with bright eyes and strong, tattooed hands. He's not here, and I *am*, and I can go wherever I want to go, while he is confined somewhere on the other side of the city. The Half Face is never going to scare me again.

# Chapter 19

## If you sing loud and clear

'You can still change your mind, if you want to.' The court attendant looks me up and down. No doubt she noticed how I wiped my clammy palms on my skirt a moment ago. 'We already have your testimony, this is more a formality than anything. Considering the past events...'

'No,' I tell her. 'It's alright, I can face him. I want to.'

We are in the same small room that I sat waiting in last time, all that time ago. It took weeks before the Half Face was flown back to Fallhallow, and even longer for a date for a new hearing to be set. Summer has long gone, and the trees outside the Justice House look barren and stark in the winter afternoon.

It's strange – now that I'm back in here, I'm not nearly as frightened as I was. The room seems completely unchanged, with the same grayish wallpaper, the wooden table, the two chairs, the cup of tea that I'm letting go cold. It smells the same too, even if I can't quite pinpoint what it is. It's almost unreal to imagine that I have sat here before, shaking with fear, as a man covered from head to toe in tattoos pointed a gun at my head. I wonder if I have remained unchanged as well.

No, I think at once. That's impossible, and I'm not sure I even want to be the same as before. This Juliet is stronger, after all. The man with the black-and-white face gave me that, at least, even if it was never his intention to do so.

I follow the court attendant out, through the painfully familiar corridors, to the courtroom. This is not the same as before; this time, there's so much security that nobody could even point a finger at me unseen, let alone slip out of tightly secured handcuffs, turn off the lights and grab me in a deadlock.

When I enter, I'm escorted to my place by a man carrying a gun. I turn my eyes away from the weapon. To distract myself, I look at my mother and sister, sitting in the gallery. They refused to let me go alone. Not this time, they had said. I'm grateful. My eyes wander to the handsome young man sitting next to them. Chris had waited for me at the airport, together with my family. I'd been surprised, shocked, choking up when he locked me in his arms after my mother and sister had hugged me.

'I was so scared for you,' he had whispered. 'God, every night I dreamed you were hurt. I don't know what to say.'

'Say nothing,' I had rasped, my own voice too unsteady to make a clear sound. At that moment, it had been enough that he was there, and holding me, and that he had missed me.

When I'm finally seated, and the guard has walked away, I know I can no longer afford to stare at my family or at Chris, or at anything else in the room. I said I had come to face him, and I convinced myself that I was ready for it. Now I have to stay true to that promise.

He's sitting in his chair behind a different table. His attorney is not the same woman as last time. I wonder if he fired her, or that she resigned herself. If she was smart, she got out before he could pull her in again, I think, remembering the flushed look she had given him. And I know, now, that he can be charming if he puts his mind to it.

He's looking straight at me, bright eyes burning like flames. Of course, I think, fighting the urge to flinch and turn my head. Of course he's still looking at me as if I'm his personal messiah. As if I belong to him. It's difficult to meet that gaze. My heartbeat increases, my breathing quickens. I clench my fists under the table, digging my fingernails into the flesh of my palms, forcing myself to remain still. I've stared longer and harder at him than this, and I got to walk away free. This should not be that much more difficult.

Still, I'm very relieved when the actual hearing begins. I don't have to do a lot, my attorney assured me beforehand. She's sitting next to me, answering the questions that need to be answered. She's my voice when I feel like I have lost mine. It just gives me more time to observe him, secretly, with glances and covert looks. What is going through that mind of his now? Does he realize what I feel? Does he still believe that I would have been his, if only he had pushed a little longer, a little harder?

'I want to talk-*ah*,' he says suddenly, interrupting the public prosecutor. Am I imagining it, or is his voice even rougher and hoarser than usual? Has he screamed a lot, in prison? 'To *Julie*. I want to speak to *her*.'

'That is out of the question, mister Sain –'

'Wait,' I say, shocking myself by speaking out of turn so suddenly. 'Can I? If I want to?'

I haven't spoken to him since the trap in Mongolia. The last words I said to him were 'Don't fight'. I had believed that was enough for me, but now I'm suddenly overtaken by a sense of urgency. If I can't finish this right, the way I would want to finish it, it will haunt me forever.

The public prosecutor hesitates. My attorney mutters: 'I'm not sure you should.'

'Yeah, I do,' I say. 'I must.'

'One minute,' the judge says, with a look of doubt on his face.

I nod and turn my attention back to the Half Face. He jumps at this chance at once.

'Julie, *Julie*,' he says. 'I miss you.'

'You don't understand, do you?' I tell him, almost gently. 'After today you will *never* see me again. I will never redeem you. You should stop waiting for me.'

'No, but you have – you are! I'm going to be good-*ah*. I am not born to be a freak; no, I will prove it to you, Julie, just wait. Just see.'

'I'm not going to wait for you.'

'But you will see anyway. I want.' He leans over the table, as far as the cuffs allow him, looking directly into my eyes. 'To be good. For *you*.'

I don't know what I was expecting, but it isn't this sinking feeling in the pit of my stomach. It isn't the weakness in my knees. I shake my head, overwhelmed by a vision in which I am once again the only thing standing between him and total chaos. I can't be that person, I realize. It would absolutely destroy me.

I'm saved from thinking up an answer by the judge, who coughs pointedly. 'That is enough. We will proceed this hearing as per the usual customs. If the prosecutor would please continue.'

The prosecutor nods, gathering her papers, and clears her throat. I fall back in my chair and listen, not even aware of what she is saying exactly. All I hear are fragments of words: an intense hostage situation, scarring circumstances for the victim, present here today, the perpetrator calling himself by the nickname 'Half Face,' newly under psychiatric treatment, prescribed drugs. All those words don't seem to cover it quite enough. It's like a tiny blanket that only partly fits the huge bulk of things that happened underneath. The victim has been found prepared to testify again, after witnessing the events of Fallhallow National Bank...

I clench my fists. I want to shout at him: *stop calling me a victim!* That's not what I am. I didn't die, I didn't get shot, I wasn't raped. The victims are the people from Fallhallow Bank.

'What's wrong?' my attorney whispers, noticing my agitated posture.

'People just can't get the label right,' I mutter. I'm as much a victim as I am a messiah. 'All I want to be is Juliet.'

As the hearing wears on, I grow more restless. There's a five minute recess, then another thirty-minutes one. People talk a lot. The Half Face's newly appointed psychiatrist sums up a list of diagnoses, none of which make any sense to me, then there's an independent doctor for a second opinion. Later on, there's another doctor, the one that took care of me once I had landed. He'd asked me questions, carefully examining my mental state of health. I had assured him, my mental state was far healthier than my physical one at that point. I was already showing signs of slight malnutrition and dehydration, caused by the combined effects of long travel in bad conditions and the minimal amount of food I had been getting. The Half Face, too, suffered from these ailments, but he had been in better shape than I was, his body already muscular and fit. He had taken it better than the following weeks in prison, I conclude, observing him silently from my seat. Now his face seems more hollow, his cheeks slightly sunken in. There's even more hair on his head now; dark, unkempt curls that seem to melt seamlessly into the black ink that has been soaked up by his scalp. Even his eyes, that at first glance seemed to be just as bright as I had always known them, seem to be a shade more dull and tired when I take another good look at them. He licks his lips often; his tongue flicking out quick as a snake, moistening the corners of his mouth. It's such a nervous gesture that it makes me nervous in turn.

Suddenly, the thought hits me: he must be terrified. All his plans failed, Black is still with him, he has endured the whippings at Oyun and Tsend's for nothing at all, and he never got to see the shaman Gansükh. And worse still: he's facing long, relentless imprisonment. I think about his story, the one he'd told me back in the hotel room in Ulaanbaatar. That little boy in a closet, both sheltered and incarcerated by the thick wooden doors that wouldn't open. I can't believe I haven't realized this before. No wonder he felt so in his element out on the steppe. On the endless sea of grass, there are no walls to close in on him.

When I am finally required to answer another question, the hearing has already been going on for hours. I think we must be almost done, though I've zoned out at least a couple of times. My attorney gives me a small nudge with her elbow, a sign for me to snap my head up.

'I'm so sorry,' I mutter. 'Please...what was the question?'

'I was asking, Miss Cunningham,' the Half Face's new attorney repeats patiently, 'if you have found my client to act unreasonably, or if you have been able to discern a certain motive to his actions.'

I stare at her. 'Why in God's name are you asking *me* this?'

'You have spent time with him privately.'

'He acted unreasonably and he had a motive. He wanted to find redemption.'

The attorney nods slowly. 'Did he mention this often?'

'Oh, all the time.'

'From the beginning?'

I try to remember the very first hours. The fear, I recall, and the pain from what I now know was a concussion. 'I think he tried to tell me something like that. He wasn't very straight.'

'And would you say all his actions were geared towards this goal?'

'Of course,' I say, feeling worn out. 'He'd endure anything to free himself. To be redeemed. Well, anything but prison.'

She asks me an unexpected question. 'Do you feel that he got close to what he wanted?'

'Got close…' I'm not sure I understand her right. 'To redeeming himself? Do you mean if I feel he should ever be let out of prison?'

'Not exactly that. But did you find him changed?'

'That's a stupid question.' But I suppose it proves that we both have changed, because I would never have dared to be so rude before Mongolia. 'All I've come to know is a man who believes there's a black spirit in his head. Well, for all I know, that's true. I'm not a doctor. I'm not his shrink, I'm definitely not a shaman and I'm not Mother Mary.' I don't even know why I am so angry all of a sudden. I fight the urge to stand up and point at the judge. Instead, I take a deep, shuddering breath and sink lower in my seat. After a moment, my heart slows down, and I shake my head. 'But if you'd ask me…if I *want* him to redeem himself…'

I fall silent. In my head, thoughts and feelings are tumbling over each other with such alarming speed that I can't untangle them enough to finish my words. Do I want it? Yes, I do. Can I say it? I don't know. But I do know what I must say to give him a fighting chance.

I moisten my lips and swallow something down before I start speaking again. 'I don't believe he will redeem himself. He cannot. The Half Face is a broken, damaged man. He is a killer. There is no redemption in that.'

The silence is palpable. I breathe out slowly, giving myself as well as everybody else the chance to let my words sink in. I'm so certain of the rightness of my words that I can feel the truth in my bones. The only way he will ever accept treatment for himself is if he harbors no secret hopes of seeing me again, of me being his Crying Madonna. All those attachments must go. He needs to believe that I do not believe in him. Perhaps that will ignite his desire to fight for himself. Perhaps it will not. In any case, I can't be a part of this anymore. I watch his face crumble, like a broken statue. His mouth moves; for a moment I think he will scream at me. But he doesn't make a sound. He just slumps down in his chair and doesn't look up anymore.

A snippet of song drifts into my memory. The nursery rhyme I sang out on the steppe, just before I spotted the white *gers* that would mean my rescue.

*If you sing loud and clear, she will hear, she will hear...*

*If it is time to rise, up to Christ, up to Christ, she will lift your soul to paradise...*

Well. I'm not that girl. I never will be.

I turn my face away. We don't look at each other anymore, not even when the hearing comes to an end, and I leave the room for good.

# Chapter 20

## For better or for good

*3 years later*

As the children run out of the classroom, finally free and heading for home, I slowly gather the drawings left on their tables. They depict grassland, hills, white, round tents. Marie-Louise even made a big, dancing woman, clad in feathers. I smile.

Today, I told them about Mongolia. Not about the country, but about me. They had known, for a while, that I was the girl from three years ago, because their parents told them, or because the other teachers sometimes mutter things when they think I'm not listening. Kids are clever that way; we think we hide things from them to protect them, but one way or another, they usually untangle a part of the truth.

And why not? I must have talked to a thousand people by now, and the story's worn thin for me. But children might as well know what this vast world has to offer – both the good things and the bad. If I can teach anyone something about resilience, or the confusing joy when a dark situation suddenly brightens, I will be happy to do so.

And it has changed me. I've known that it would since the very beginning, but it has not been until this day that I realize in what ways I have been altered. First, I believed that the changes were for the worst: that I would never sleep again, that darkness was too much to bear, that I almost heard him breathing down my neck. I believed I would never feel safe again. But slowly, gradually, I began to understand that he had given me a gift. Not intentionally, but well, the best gifts usually come unexpectedly.

What he gave me was an intense, burning need for self-reliance. So I stopped going to a therapist and took up self-defense classes instead. When I could throw a man twice my size on the floor, whether he grabbed me from behind or up front, I moved on to wilderness survival courses. When you've been out in an endless, empty land, the hunger, the cold and the lack of shelter are not things you easily forget.

Finally, I took lessons in gun control. This was the hardest thing by far. Just the sound of that metal click upon loading a bullet made me want to vomit. When I got to hold one for the first time, and shoot it, I could only think of poor Batzorig's bulging eyes. The fear they had held, as he realized what the Half Face was going to do. How he would *die*, far away, in the steppe.

Guns are cruel. They're just metal cases with an iron marble in it, but they will devastate lives in a few seconds. Yet guns are only as cruel as the people that yield them. They can also save lives. I had to learn this again, before I stopped cringing whenever I saw an armed police officer.

I collect the drawings in a special file folder, kept in my desk drawer. By the end of the year, I will hand them out to the kids again, along with all their other pieces of art. I will pick one out for each of them, and frame them, as an end-of-the-year gift. Marie-Louise might just get her shaman woman framed.

When I get home, there's a letter waiting for me. It looks like Mom's handwriting, but that's weird. Why would she write me a letter? Who still writes letters at all?

I open the envelope quickly, pulling out a double-folded piece of paper. The letters are tight, small, in black ink. Definitely not Mom's. I flip over the sheet of paper. There's no name. Just words – lots of words.

With a growing fear of dread, I let my eyes move up again. *To my Julie...*

For the love of God! I nearly drop the paper, staring at the abbreviation of my name with what is now a definite sense of horror. How did he ever manage to get my address? What sick person in that prison where he's locked away thought it was a good idea to violate my privacy?

Wait – I look at the date, scribbled in the top right corner. It was two years ago. Confused, I turn the letter over again, but there are no other clues.

I throw the letter on my coffee table and try to calm myself down, focusing on the familiar routine of making a cup of tea: boiling the water, picking the tea bag, pouring the tea in my cup. When I have no more excuses left, I drop onto my couch and curl my legs underneath me, the steaming cup next to me on the coffee table. The letter is here now. I've opened it, and I know that I will not be able to put it out of my mind if I decide to throw it away unread.

No, I will have to read it now. I curse myself for it, but unfold the piece of paper and start at the beginning.


*To my Julie,*

*I'm writing to you, following the advice of my therapist. I don't believe he means for me to actually send letters to you, but I want you to read them all the same. I want you to be the only one who knows all my secrets.*

*You may not care to understand, but these days in confinement are lonely. Some days, I hardly get to speak to anyone, let alone have a decent conversation. If you find it in your heart, please write me back. I have included an envelope with the address, my prisoner's number and even a stamp.*

*Not a day goes by without remembering you, Julie. I think about you so often that it seems like you are with me in my cell. Sometimes, I can even  smell you. The scent of your hair, the warmth of your body against mine. Those moments are my comfort. I close my eyes and imagine what could have*


'God damn it, no!' I put the letter away and stare up, chills running over my arms and back. It feels like my chest is squeezing shut, making me uncomfortably breathless. I can't read this. I do not want to know what he imagines, alone in his cell. I should never be burdened with that knowledge.

I grab a matchbox from the kitchen, light the match and hold it against the paper. It burns quickly and hungrily, eating the unread letters alive. Now I will never have to know what insane, deranged fantasies he has created about us.

When there's nothing left but brittle, black pieces of paper, I call my mother. I tell her what just happened, and to my surprise, she falls strangely silent.

'Mom?' I say. 'What's going on?'

'I'm sorry, Juliet.' Ever since my phone call from Ulaanbaatar, she has stopped calling me Julie. 'I felt you should see it. Just in case you wanted to read it. Then, if...if you did, I would give you the rest of the stack.'

'Stack, what stack? What are you talking about?'

'The letters. He wrote you, oh, hundreds of them. It started two years ago, and he just went on. Twice a week, sometimes. I thought you'd...rather not know about them. But then I thought...What if she does?'

I can't speak for a full thirty seconds. My head is spinning. 'You're telling me you have all these letters, hidden away somewhere? He *wrote* to me? *All* this time?'

'Yes.'

'I can't believe it. Why – did you...' I struggle to find the right words. 'Did you just decide to randomly send me one now?'

'It's the first one. I thought it would help you make up your mind – I was going to tell you, Juliet, honestly; I had put the letter by the front door to remind myself to send it, but your sister put it on the pile of the regular mail...I'm sorry. Are you very upset?'

'Yes, I'm very upset! How could you just keep this from me?'

'I wanted to protect you. What else?'

'I don't need protection,' I say slowly. 'Certainly not from him. I should have known.'

'I'm so sorry.'

'So, what now?' I ask, moistening my lips. Despite my brave words, my hands are shaking. I drop back on the couch to steady myself. 'What am I supposed to think of this? How many did he write after this?'

'Hundreds. Like I said. He seems to be completely...'

'Obsessed?' I laugh bitterly. 'Yeah, mom, that's what he is. He asked me to *write back*. There's a frigging envelope with his address and prisoner number and everything. Do you know what it means that he kept writing me anyway? He's not going to put me out of his mind until he is dead!'

'So...so you don't want to see the other letters, then? Juliet?'

'I don't know!' My head suddenly feels twice as heavy, as if it's swelling to contain all the conflicting thoughts springing up. Things that I thought I'd left in Mongolia, with that last, weird kiss we shared. 'Now that I know they're here...Maybe I *should* know what he's written.'

'Tell you what,' Mom says. 'Why don't you just read his latest letter, and then decide if you want to see the rest.'

'The latest? When was that sent?'

'About a week ago.'

'A week.' I had hardly thought about him this week; not until I made my story a school assignment today. It's painful to imagine that he still thinks about me enough to write me letters, even if I never replied. Suddenly weary, I close my eyes. 'Okay. That sounds good. Can you bring it over now?'

'If you're really sure.'

'Yeah. It's fine. I want to see it.'

After we hang up, I don't move for a full five minutes. My belly is aching. A letter is not the same as being confronted with the writer, I remind myself. A letter can't hurt me at all. But a letter from just a week ago is also something other than a stray one sent two years back. I can't deny that, either.

When Mom arrives, she hands me the envelope. I notice his handwriting immediately: this time, Mom didn't bother to change the envelope. She doesn't stay long. I guess she realizes that I need time to do this alone. For better or for worse, these are probably words I need to read.

I open the letter and stare at its content.

*Juliet,*

*Despite all my pleadings, you have never once responded to my letters. I assume, therefore, that you do not wish to correspond with me on any level.*

*I remember you telling me that I cannot at the same time redeem and excuse myself. Those words still ring out clearly in my head. Of course, you were right. These last few months, I feel like Black has slipped into a coma, and every day I am less wary that he will emerge again. And every passing day, I strive to accomplish small victories: I don't get upset anymore when the warden is rude to me. I accept my daily rhythm within these confinements, and try to find enjoyment in the little things, such as the books I am allowed to have in my cell. The latest of these victories is the regaining of my own name. I wear it like I would wear an ill-fitting shoe - uncomfortably - but perhaps I will one day slip into it with ease, and not even realize it.*

*During sessions, I try to drag up every scrap of goodness that I can find within myself, and I talk about you. So you see, you were mistaken; I do need you. But I will not be writing to you anymore - the memory will have to be enough for me from now on, and I feel that I have enough to fuel me. You have changed me - for better and for good.*

*So, I will no longer try to find you, Juliet. But I will leave you with one final promise. I will find the redemption that you believed was beyond my grasp. I will be better each day, until there comes a time when good has become a second skin. As my reward, I will picture you smiling at me without reserve; without fear in your eyes.*

*Goodbye, Julie.*

*Liam St. James.*

# Epilogue

The visitor's room is small and empty. Just a table, two chairs, and a large glass window, that enables the ever-present guards to observe everything that is going on inside.

When they let me in, I am nervous. He's not here yet; they said he would be fetched in a minute, and it gives me a chance to accustom myself to this new, cold place. The entire prison feels claustrophobic, with doors that have to be unlocked everywhere, narrow corridors, new doors... But that is a good thing, I remind myself. After all, it must be nearly impossible to break out of Fallhallow Penitentiary.

They tell me nobody comes for him, ever. They tell me he is lonely. That it makes him suffer. They even got him on anti-depressants for a while, afraid he would otherwise do something to end his own life.

I sit down on one of the chairs, facing the empty one in front of me. I can't stay long. I don't even know if I have anything to say.

When the door opens and he is brought in, I rise at once. His face changes as fast as a strike of lighting. There's bafflement in those bright blue eyes, and even apprehension. Seeing that suddenly wipes my own fear from my heart. I lift my chin and find his gaze.

'Hello, Liam,' I say. 'I've come to see what you've made of yourself.'

# More books by

# Lands Atlantic Publishing

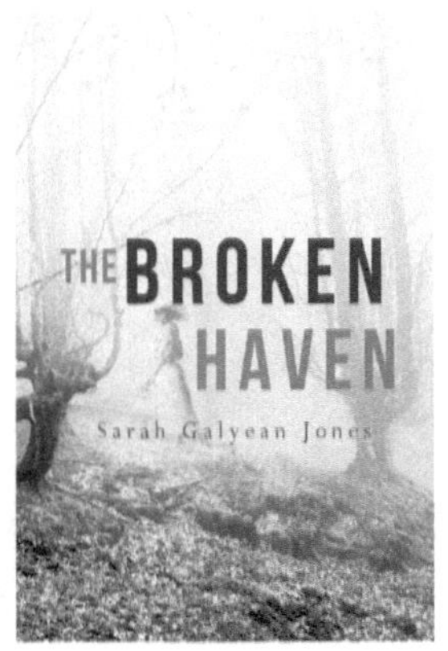

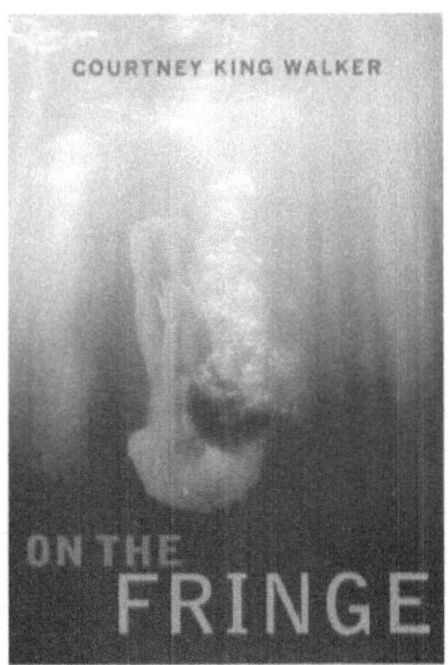